The Case of the Saddle House Robbery

The Case of the Saddle House Robbery

John R. Erickson

Illustrations by Gerald L. Holmes

Viking

VIKING
Published by the Penguin Group
Penguin Putnam Books for Young Readers,
345 Hudson Street, New York, New York 10014, U.S.A.
Penguin Books Ltd, 27 Wrights Lane, London W8 5TZ, England
Penguin Books Australia Ltd, Ringwood, Victoria, Australia
Penguin Books Canada Ltd, 10 Alcorn Avenue,
Toronto, Ontario, Canada M4V 3B2
Penguin Books (N.Z.) Ltd, 182-190 Wairau Road, Auckland 10, New Zealand

Penguin Books Ltd, Registered Offices: Harmondsworth, Middlesex, England

Published simultaneously by Viking and Puffin Books, divisions
of Penguin Putnam Books for Young Readers, 2000

1 3 5 7 9 10 8 6 4 2

The Library of Congress has cataloged the Puffin edition as follows
Erickson, John R., date
Hank the Cowdog : the case of the Saddle House robbery / John R. Erickson ;
illustrations by Gerald L. Holmes.
p.   cm. — (Hank the Cowdog ; 35)
ISBN: 0-14-130678-5 (pbk.)
1. Ranch life—West (U.S.)—Fiction 2. Dogs—West (U.S.)—Fiction.
I. Holmes, Gerald L., II. Title.
PS3555.R428 H335 2000 813'.54—dc21 99-056337

Viking ISBN 0-670-88890-7

Hank the Cowdog® is a registered trademark of John R. Erickson.

Printed in the United States of America
Set in New Century Schoolbook

To Jody Logsdon

CONTENTS

The Case of the Saddle House Robbery

CHAPTER ONE

The Earth Is Plunged into Darkness

It's me again, Hank the Cowdog. Let's get right to the point of this case. Our ranch was visited, struck, and robbed by a saddle thief.

Saddle thieves steal saddles, right? That's what this one did. Even though we had been warned, even though I was on the case from the start, the clever rogue managed to . . .

This will be painful. See, I had him cornered in the saddle shed, yet somehow . . . somehow I let him slip away. Maybe you find that hard to believe. Me too. Hard to believe and even harder to accept. I failed my ranch, that's the bottom line, and it almost got me . . .

1

But let me hasten to add that he *cheated*. Who would expect a saddle thief to appear in broad daylight? Thieves are supposed to strike in the darkness of night, but this guy came in the middle of the day. It was a dirty sneaky trick, and no dog would have . . .

Oh, and did I mention the chocolate candy? Maybe not. That was really a low-down dirty trick, using a dog's natural love of . . . well, yummy chocolate . . .

I'm not sure I can go on with this. It's too painful.

It happened in the winter, as I recall. Yes, of course it was, the middle of winter. Cold mornings. Short days. Long nights. That's an accurate description of winter on the ranch.

Me, I was sick of long nights and short days. I mean, the sun didn't come up until almost eight o'clock! That was shocking, disgraceful. Those of us who work for a living, and who take pride in working long hours, get impatient when the day doesn't start until eight o'clock.

Those were Drover hours. He loved our winter schedule. It allowed him to sleep his life away. I, however, had better things to do with my life, and on that particular morning at approximately 0716, I decided to take matters in my own hands. Of course I had no way of knowing . . .

Acting on a sudden impulse, I decided to bark up the sun at 0730 instead of waiting until 0800. Pretty bold, huh? You bet it was, but I'd had it up to *here* with gloom and darkness and short working days. By George, we needed more daylight and I was just the guy to handle that situation.

And so it was that I left Mister Snore-and-Squeak on his gunnysack and began my march toward that little hill just east of the house, the same hill where I barked up the sun every morning of the year.

As you might have guessed, it was dark, very dark, and in the gloomy black of the black gloominess I collided with something—something hairy, warm, and alive, possibly one of the many varieties of Night Monster that roam the ranch at night. We have many of them: Bush Monsters, Shadow Monsters, Thunder Monsters, Moaning Wind Monsters . . . and they're all pretty scary.

It caught me by surprise. Perhaps I had been so preoccupied with my thoughts that I had, well, neglected to check my instruments. See, I had been running on Smell-o-radar and should have picked up a signal, but somehow I'd missed it.

And I ran into this Hairy Thing in the inky darkness and . . . okay, let's be honest. It gave me quite a scare. I'm no chicken liver when it comes to defending my ranch against monsters, but I don't go shopping for trouble either.

Those monsters can be ferocious. A guy needs to pick his fights pretty carefully. Bumping into them in the dark is bad business.

It sent a shockwave all the way out to the end of my tail. I bristled my hair and leaped several feet to the left. Right. Who cares? I leaped, that's the point.

"Halt! Stop! Who goes there? Stop in the name of the law and reach for the sky. I've got this place surrounded!"

Pretty tough, huh? You bet it was, but that's the way you have to talk to those monsters. Give 'em an inch and they'll take every nickel.

Having issued the Halt-Stop-Who-Goes-There, I waited for some kind of response. If I was lucky, the monster would run. They do that sometimes, just run away and vanish in the night and you never see 'em again. But sometimes they don't and a guy never knows . . .

I waited, poised and cocked and . . . well, ready to go streaking for the front porch, if events, uh, got out of control. (Monsters never follow dogs to front porches, don't you see. I don't know why, but it's true.) But then I heard a voice.

"Mmmm, my goodness, I think I've just been

4

stepped on by Hankie the Wonder Dog."

The air hissed out of my lungs. My whole body went limp. I almost fainted with relief. You probably thought it was a ferocious Night Monster, right? Nope. It was just a cat—Pete the Barncat, to be exact, my least-favorite character on the ranch. Have we discussed cats? Maybe not. I don't like 'em, have no use for 'em at all.

"What are you doing out here, you little sneak? I thought you were a . . . that is, I picked up an odd unidentified sound and rushed right over to check it out."

"Did you now?"

"Yes I did, Kitty, and at this very moment, even as we speak, I am checking you out."

"My goodness, Hankie, I'm so impressed."

"No you're not. You're too dumb to be impressed. You're just a dumb cat, Pete. Why are you lurking out here in the dark?"

I glared daggers into the void of blackness from which his voice had come. I couldn't actually see him, don't you know, and more or less had to glare where to guess.

He spoke again. "I'm over here, Hankie. You're glaring at a rock."

I whirled around and beamed my glare at the new location. "I know exactly where you are, Kitty, and don't try to dodge the question. What are you doing out here?"

"Well, Hankie, these winter nights are so long, I sometimes wake up before daylight and walk around."

"I see. And you think I'm not aware that the nights are long in the winter, is that your point? Ha! For your information, Kitty, our Security Division keeps very careful records on all that stuff."

"That wasn't my point, Hankie."

"Great. What was your point? You're boring me, Pete. Could we hurry this along? I'm a very busy dog."

"I was walking around in the dark. That's all."

"Oh, so that's it. And you think I wasn't smart enough to have figured that out on my own, huh? Hey, Pete, I knew exactly what you were doing, and I knew exactly why you were doing it. Shall I go on?"

"By all means, Hankie, but I'm over here. You're talking to a tree."

I whirled 24 degrees to the left and aimed a gaze of purest steel at him. "Okay, try this on, Pete. You were walking around in the dark because it was dark."

"Very impressive, Hankie."

"Hold your applause, Kitty, I'm not through. It

was dark this morning because the sun wasn't up, because it's winter, Pete. Don't you get it? No sun, no sunrise. No sun, no daylight. No sun equals darkness. That's why you were walking around in the dark."

"That's amazing, Hankie. And you figured that out yourself?"

I couldn't hold back a little chuckle. "Heh. You cats have no idea what goes on around here while you sleep. But I'm still not finished. Wait until you hear this last part. It just might knock your socks off."

"Ooooo! I can hardly wait. But I'm over here, Hankie."

"Right." I whirled 12 degrees to the left and gave him a stern glare. "For your information, Kitty, at this very moment I'm on my way to Sunrise Hill, where I will bark up the sun thirty minutes ahead of schedule, thus adding thirty minutes of daylight to the day. What do you think of that?"

He gasped. "I think something just happened to my socks."

"Ha! Didn't I tell you? I blew 'em right off, didn't I?"

"You certainly did, Hankie. And you think you can bark up the sun early today?"

"Hey Kitty, this is my ranch. If the sun wants to rise on my ranch, it'll rise when I tell it to. We need more daylight, yes? So I'll bark it up thirty minutes early. It's a simple process."

"How fun. But Hankie, I thought J. T. Cluck crowed up the sun every morning."

I froze. "What? Who told you that?"

"Well, maybe J.T. told me, but I've also watched him doing it—many times."

"Lies, Pete, lies. Number one, the sun must be *barked* up, not *crowed* up. Number two, it takes a dog to bark up the sun. Number three, the sun pays no attention to a silly, squawking rooster. And number four, J. T. Cluck is a fraud, a cheat, a liar, and a lying fraudulent cheat. He has nothing to do with the rising of the sun, period."

I heard the cat gasp. "My goodness, Hankie, I didn't know all this. And you're going to bark up the sun earlier than usual this morning?"

"That's correct, Kitty. Then you won't have to lurk around in the darkness, and I won't have to wonder what you're doing."

"I'll be watching, Hankie."

"Do that, Pete, and feel free to take notes, if you wish. It might improve that tiny mind of yours."

"Mmmmm yes, but I'm over here, Hankie. You're talking to the tree again."

That did it. This cat was trying to play games with me and I'd taken all the trash I could stand from him, so instead of answering or adjusting my position, I issued a growl and launched myself into . . .

BONK!

. . . the middle of a stupid tree, a very large stupid tree, which had looked very much like a cat lurking in the darkness, only it wasn't. I don't know how the little pest had managed to . . . phooey.

Did it hurt? You bet it did. It hurt big-time, scratched the soft, leathery portion of my nose and brought tears to my eyes, but they were mostly

tears of joy, for I'd had the pleasure of . . . never mind.

It hurt.

Then I heard his voice again, somewhere in the darkness. (Obviously he had been moving around, trying to confuse me.) "Sorry, Hankie. I tried to warn you."

I paused for a moment, searching my mind for a stinging, witty reply that would wound him even more than the tree had wounded my nose. After thirty seconds of really heavy concentration, I gave it up and had to settle for "Shut up, cat."

And with that, I whirled around and marched . . . bush? . . . marched into a wandering bush that had somehow . . . hey, don't forget, it was *very dark* out there, and that was the whole point of my mission, right? It was so dreadfully dark that no dog in the whole world could have seen where he was going, and before somebody got hurt, I needed to get that sun barked up. Right away. Chop-chop.

And so it was that I managed to snatch a moral victory out of the jowls of defeat and left the cat sitting in the ruins of his own shambles.

I don't know why I'd even bothered to speak to him. Trying to communicate with cats was a waste of time, a teetotal waste of time, and I had much more important things to do than . . . boy, that tree had really messed up my nose. It throbbed with every step.

Kitty-Kitty would pay for this.

I finally managed to push Pete's nonsense out of my mind and poured all my vast mental insurgencies into the morning's mission: barking up the sun thirty minutes ahead of schedule.

It was a very important mission. The world was lost in a great blinding darkness. Only the Head of Ranch Security could save it, and I just happened to be the right dog for that job.

Little did I know that . . . hmmm, better not say.

CHAPTER TWO

I Bark Up Cannibals, Not the Sun

Holding my head at a proud angle, I marched myself in an easterly direction, across the caliche drive in front of the house, past that young cottonwood tree that Sally May had raised from a mere twig, and on out into the deep darkness of the Home Pasture, until at last I came to Point Zero: Sunrise Hill.

I reached Point Zero at precisely . . . whatever the time, it was precisely the time I arrived there and that was close enough, considering all the nonsense and follyrot I'd had to endure from Sally May's precious kitty.

I had never understood what she saw in that little schemer. Oh well.

I marched myself out to the easternmost point

12

of the hill and went right into my Preparations and Warm-Ups for the big event. A lot of your ordinary dogs wouldn't have gone to the trouble of prepping themselves for this job, but I did. And I guess it wouldn't hurt if I revealed the procedure I followed here.

I started by taking thirteen deep breaths, one for each day of the week. Wait. One for each day of the week, plus six extras for Tuesday. Why the six extra for Tuesday? I'm sorry, but I'm not at liberty to reveal that information. All I can tell you is that we were following charts and graphs that showed Tuesday falling between Monday and Wednesday.

Okay, I did the deep breathing so-forths, then went plunging right into a series of exercises, and once again, we run up against the Wall of Secrecy, which surrounds so much of our work in the Security Division. I can't describe the exercises. Sorry. I can tell you only that they were calculated to direct a tremendous energy field into my barking procedure.

You see, the task of barking the sun above the horizon required huge amounts of ozmottic energy and . . . I really can't say any more about it. No kidding. If this information fell into the wrong hands . . . well, think about it. We could never be sure who was raising the sun. It might be going up in the middle of the day or the middle of the night. It could be very bad.

Okay. I zipped through my checklist of exercises and routines and so forth, until at last I felt prepared for the awesome task that awaited me. I turned myself in a precise east-west orientation, stiffened my tail, took three deep breaths, and began barking—and fellers, we're talking about deep heavy-duty ozmottic barkings, the kind that rumble into the distance and cause full-grown cottonwood trees to rattle and shake.

Yes sir, we had launched ourselves into some serious barking.

I barked and I barked.

Hmmm.

Then I *barked* and I *barked*.

Hmmmm.

Then I threw everything I had into it, and I ***barked*** and I ***barked*** and I **BARKED!**

You probably think that the, uh, sun came shooting up from below the horizon. I had kind of expected that myself, to be honest about it, but . . . something had . . . once in a while we get the wrong mix of . . .

Okay, maybe the sun didn't exactly come skipping into view, but I hasten to add that I did notice a few strink peaks of light on the horizon . . . pink streaks, I should say, on the horizon, a sure indication that, while the sun may have been too lazy and dumb to leap into view, it had . . . uh . . . heard my massive barkings and was at least thinking of . . .

It didn't go just exactly as I had planned, but even more important was the fact that my amazing burst of barking seemed to have triggered a mysterious echo effect. Yes sir. I'd never heard anything quite like it. See, after launching three huge rounds of barking, I paused to catch my breath and to . . . well, to watch the sun leap into the air, which we already know didn't happen.

But what *did* happen was that, suddenly and all at once, I began hearing my own barks returning! I was amazed by this at first, but then it began to make sense. Your high-energy ozmottic barkings will sometimes travel hundreds of miles, strike a solid object such as a mountain range or a grain elevator, and then return to the ear of the barker.

You've heard of your radar and your sonar? Same deal, high-energy pulses of ozmottic so-forth bouncing off a whatever and coming back.

But the amazing thing about this deal was that the barks kept coming. According to our records at Data Control, we had launched . . . let's see, 2+2+3=7 . . . we had launched exactly seven barks. But do you know how many barks came back? Not seven, as you might have guessed, but *eleven*. Yes sir, we had launched seven and eleven had returned.

This was very strange, very strange indeed. We put Data Control to work on it right away, crunching the numbers and searching for a pattern here. At last we got the solution. Here's what it said, and this is an exact quote:

"Seven-come-eleven. They must be shooting dice."

Shooting dice? That made no sense at all. Who or whom or what was shooting dice? In a flash I punched in the codes and commands for "Retread"—"Retry," actually—but we came up with the same message.

Hmmmm. There was something fishy going on here and I had to get to the bottom of the barrel. It was bad luck that Data Control had failed to answer the vital questions, and now I had to follow it up on my own.

I issued a Test Bark, then cocked my right ear and listened. Two barks returned. I issued a second Test Bark. Three barks returned. Was there a pattern here? No. I didn't know what we had, only that it was pretty derned mysterious.

I issued a third Test Bark and got one back this time, but aha! This time I picked up a crucial piece of information. The returning bark seemed closer than the ones before. I fired off a fourth and fifth Test Bark, and yes, the pattern continued.

Those returning barks were definitely getting closer.

How could this be? What could be causing the echoing barks to . . . wait. Something moved in the darkness. Yes, right out there in front of me, near the base of Sunrise Hill. A shadowy form seemed to be . . . two shadowy forms seemed to be creeping up the hill in my . . .

HUH?

Glittering yellow eyes?

I was beginning to feel a little uneasy about this. I mean, echoes don't have glittering yellow eyes, right? Echoes don't even have eyes, right? So what the heck . . . and echoes don't have voices either, but all at once I was pretty sure that I heard . . .

"Uh! That you, Hunk? Pretty foolish you come out in black dark and play Talk Back Bark with most dangerous guys!"

Hunk? Talk Back Bark?

I cut my eyes from side to side. Data Control was flashing a warning light. Okay, it was all coming clear now. Remember all that stuff about "seven-come-eleven" and "shooting dice"? That was nothing but a garbage report from Data Control.

What we had confronting us now had nothing to
do with shooting dice or high-energy echoes.

What we had confronting us now was a whole
lot worse—Rip and Snort, the coyote brothers.
Have we discussed Rip and Snort? There had been
times in my career when I had shared some laughs
with them, but there had been other times when
I'd gotten the feeling that they wanted to . . . well,
to eat me.

And now it appeared that they had broken my
codes and intermessed my messages, followed my

barking patterns, and traced them back to ME.

Me, standing alone on Funeral Hill. Me, away from the safety of the house.

I swallowed a big lump in my throat, then addressed them in their own coyalect diote . . . coyote dialect, shall we say, a primitive grunting version of Universal Doglish. "Hey, Rip and Snort, how's it going, fellas? Nice morning for a walk, huh?"

"Ha! Big phooey on walk. Nice morning for fight. Hunk ready for big noisy fight?"

"I . . . uh . . . no, not really." I began backing away. "See, I was just . . . did you guys hear about the big dice game? Yeah, big dice game. You know, 'seven-come-eleven' and all that stuff. I know for a fact that you guys love to gamble."

"Us guys love to fight, beat up dummy ranch dog, kick and bite and scratch, oh boy." They were getting closer. I could smell them now. Boy, did they stink. "How come Hunk stand on hill, in plainest sight, and bark louder and loudest?"

"Well, I . . . if you must know, Snort, I was trying to bark up the sun a little earlier than usual." I continued backing away, but this time they noticed. I heard them growling.

"Hunk not try sneaking back to house and boom-boom."

"Me? Sneak back to the house? Ha, ha. Not me, guys, no sir. Really. No, I have to stay out here until I get that old sun barked up."

By this time they were right in front of me and I could see the outline of their sharp noses and sharp ears. I must admit that the sight of them, and the smell too, sent shivers of dread down my spine. I couldn't believe I had gotten myself into this mess. Why hadn't I . . . oh well, it was too late to spill the milk.

Snort looked me over and then spoke. "Hunk barking up sun?"

"Sure. That's one of my jobs on this outfit. I bark up the sun every morning."

That drew a big laugh from the cannibals. "Ha! Hunk got big stupid in head, not have enough bark for punch hole in wet paper sack."

"Oh yeah? Tell that to the sun, Snort, because it comes up every morning when I bark at it . . . well, except this morning, and for some reason it didn't work."

"Didn't work 'cause Hunk have weenie bark."

"Weenie bark! Are you kidding me? Oh, I get it. You're thinking of Drover, and yes, you might describe his bark as a weenie bark. But see, I'm not Drover." They stared at me with empty eyes. "I'm not, honest. I'm not Drover and

I've never been Drover. Therefore . . ."

"Therefore Hunk talk too much." He clubbed me over the head with his paw. BONK! "Hunk have weenie bark and not bark up sun."

"Okay, fine. But if I don't bark up the sun, why do you think it comes up every morning, huh? You can't answer that, can you?"

They exchanged wicked glances and grinned. Then Snort puffed himself up to his full height and tapped himself on the chest. "Rip and Snort howl up sun, not dummy ranch dog with weenie bark."

"Oh yeah? Let's see you do it."

The cannibals exchanged grins and nodded their heads. "Ha! Hunk fixing to see. Better watch real close."

The brothers turned and faced the east. Well, they had that part right, facing east instead of north or west. They sat down on their haunches, puffed themselves up with big gulps of air, and started launching their famous "Coyote Howl-Up-the-Sun Song" toward the eastern horizon.

Have we discussed that song? Maybe not. It was a special coyote song they used for this one big event. It wasn't quite as bad as most of the trash they sang, but it was bad enough. Here's how it went, word for word and note for note.

The Coyote Howl-Up-the-Sun Song

Sun get up
Off your duff
We cannibals order the start of day.
Shake a leg,
Out of bed.
Or else we will have to get mad.
That's bad.

Well, they finished their noise, and you know what? It was still as dark as the inside of a cow. The sun wasn't coming up.

This pleased me, of course, but I didn't dare say a word. Snort mumbled something about "dummy sun," then he and Rip reloaded their lungs with air, and went back to work. This time, they skipped the singing and went to straight howling. They howled so hard and loud, they both collapsed on the ground.

Snort called me over. "Maybe Hunk better help howl up stupid sun."

"Now you're talking. Okay, guys, the gloves come off now. Let's give it the full load this time."

And so it was that . . .

BONK!

CHAPTER THREE

Code Three!

Snort clubbed me over the head again. "Hunk not give orders to coyote brothers."

"Well, sure, but . . ."

The important thing is that they dragged themselves off the ground and got into their howling stances. We were ready. I counted to three and we cut loose with the most amazing barrage of howling and barking that had ever been heard on the ranch. It was very impressive.

We barked and howled and filled that whole valley with . . .

You probably think the sun leaped over the horizon, and suddenly the night was transformed into daily broadlight. Not exactly.

You might not believe this, but the sun resisted

all our howling and barking. We barked and howled ourselves into puddles of hair—exhausted puddles of exhausted hair—and the idiot sun refused to come up!

All three of us collapsed in a heap on the . . . well, on the ground, of course. Where else would three exhausted guys collapse? We were bushed, spent, defeated, light-headed, and gasping for breath.

I was the first to squeak. *Speak*, I should say, although I must admit that it came out as a kind of squeak. "Boys, I don't want to alarm you, but we may be witnessing some kind of universal calamity here. The sun has resisted our best efforts. We have to face the possibility that it will never rise again. Never ever."

I heard them gulp in the darkness. That expressed it pretty well. For reasons that we didn't understand, those pink streaks didn't seem to be getting any brighter. The world had been plunged into permanent darkness.

My thoughts were interrupted just then by a squawky sound coming from headquarters. I cocked my ear and listened. Rip and Snort cocked their respective ears and listened.

I broke the silence. "Oh, it's J. T. Cluck, the local rooster. He thinks he can squawk up the sun, but of course he doesn't realize . . ."

I'm afraid I can't reveal what happened next. It was too outrageous. You'd never believe it. Even I didn't believe it, and it happened before my very eyes.

Let's skip it and move along with the story.

Nothing happened, okay? I didn't go out to bark up the sun that morning. I stayed on my gunny-sack bed, and I didn't run into Rip and Snort. And most important, we didn't throw ourselves into the effort of . . .

Okay, here's the deal. Mere seconds after J. T. Cluck began his squawking routine . . . *the sun came up!* My cannibal pals and I, we who had spent the last half hour barking and howling ourselves into exhaustion, were shocked. If we hadn't been so tired, we might have also been outraged. I mean, the very idea . . .

For a whole entire minute, none of us could speak. Then Snort said, "Hunk make big mess out of coyote job."

"Me? Hey, I gave it my best shot. It wasn't my fault. The rooster got lucky, that's all."

"Uh. Then Hunk better go back and *fix* rooster."

I stared at them. "Fix the rooster?"

"Beat him up. Rip and Snort madder and maddest for losing sun-bark-up deal."

"I agree. It's the only course left to us. If someone doesn't give him a thrashing, he's liable to think he actually did what we saw him do—which we all know was impossible and outrageous. Roosters can't crow up the sun." The brothers nodded. "Only dogs and coyotes can do that." The brothers nodded. "And the fact that we failed and he succeeded is further proof that this has gone far enough." The brothers nodded. "I'll take care of it, guys."

I struggled to my feet. My knees were still shaking from all the effort we had put into our noble attempt. I started walking toward the west, when all at once I was overwhelmed by emotion.

"Fellers, it was a great campaign. Even though we failed, we gave it our best effort, and it was a real pleasure . . ."

They were asleep—sprawled out in the pasture and conked out. Even so, I finished my thought.

"If you fleabags hadn't come along, I would have had that sun barked up thirty minutes ago. You dumbbells couldn't bark your way out of a spider web. You know why we got beat by a rooster? Because you're a couple of slackers, that's why, and the next time I need to bark up the sun . . ."

Snort raised his head and glared at me. "What Hunk say?"

"I said . . . hey, you guys were awesome. The next

time we try to bark up the sun, by George, we'll do it right, huh? You bet we will. See you down the road." I waved good-bye and hurried away. Under my breath, I added, "Fleabags."

I ran back to headquarters. Even though I was operating on the very last of my energy reserves, I took the time to visit the chicken house. Heh heh. J.T. was standing out in front. Fifteen deranged hens were hovering nearby, gasping and holding their wings in front of their bodies and clucking about J.T.'s latest accomplishment.

The minute he saw me, a grin spread across his beak and he began mouthing off. "You know, pooch, if you'd make a little less noise in the mornings, I'd have an easier time crowing up that sun."

One bite of his tail feathers solved that little problem. Then I ran into Pete, who also made the mistake of mouthing off. "Well, Hankie, your little plan didn't work too well, did it? Just darn the luck." Heh heh. He soon found it necessary to run for his life and climb a tree.

Well, that took care of that. Having settled all accounts with all the local frauds and imposters, I returned to my bedroom under the gas tanks, did three turns around my gunnysack bed, and collapsed. All was well in the world. I had ... uh ... participated in the rising of the sun, shall we say,

had thrashed a smart-aleck rooster, and humbled the cat.

I drifted off into sleep's warm embrace, knowing that I had done my part to make the world a better, safer place.

It must have been ten or fifteen minutes later when my ears began picking up a new and odd sound. My left ear shot up, twisted around, and homed in on the sound. Holy smokes, *we had an unidentified vehicle approaching the ranch!*

I leaped out of my bed and began barking the alarm. "Get up, Drover, we've got a Code Three coming into headquarters! Get into Bark-the-Car Formation and let's check it out."

The little mutt lifted his head and cracked open his eyes. "Gosh, is it serious?"

"Every unauthorized penetration of the ranch is serious, Drover, and some are even more serious than others. Get into formation and let's move out."

He did, and we went swooping around the south side of the house. Boy, you should have seen us! Twenty-five yards out, we began a withering barrage of barking. Seconds later, we had the vehicle surrounded and had forced it to stop in front of the house.

Pretty impressive, huh? You bet it was, but that was just the beginning. Once we had this guy pulled over and stopped, I sprang into action and began shouting orders.

"Okay, Drover, prepare to Mark Tires! You take the right side. I've got the left side."

"Should we give 'em a Full Mark or a Short Squirt?"

"Short Squirt. We haven't run a check on these people and we don't know their intentions. It could be dangerous, so, yes, dart in there and do a Short

Squirt. We can always go back later and do a better job. Move out!"

You should have seen us in action. It was poetry in motion. All our skill as dogs, all our training, all our dedication to duty came out in this exercise. Drover swooped in and knocked out both tires on the right side, and I've got to give the little mutt credit. He held his fire, took careful aim, and placed the ordinance in the target area.

Sometimes he doesn't do it that well, you know. I've seen times when he's lost control and started firing wild shots in all directions, but this time he delivered the goods.

Me? Well, I stepped up to the left front tire and *blasted* it. Hey, when you hit a tire with such force and accuracy that it makes the hubcap ring, you know you've done the job right. And that's just what I did, made that rascal ring like a bell.

I was tempted to linger and give it another round, but I had called for the Short Squirt Procedure, and timing is very important in this maneuver. If I had lingered even two or three seconds, it would have thrown off all our timing, which might have . . . I don't know what might have happened, but it could have had serious consequences. My buddy was working the other side, following a very precise timing schedule, and I had to do the same.

Teamwork, see. We're part of a team, an elite team of highly trained dogs who . . . all at once this seems kind of boring. Let's move on.

Okay, I lobbed a blast into Tire #1 and ran at full speed to Tire #2. The second tire is always the tougher in a Two-Tire Situation. For one thing, a guy has to reload on the run. For another thing, you've got the problem of exhaustion and dehydration. And finally, by the time we get to the second tire, we sometimes draw enemy fire.

See, the left side of the vehicle is more dangerous than the right, because the steering wheel and so forth are on the left side, and that's where the driver sits. Are you getting the picture? When we draw fire, it usually comes from the driver.

I know this is pretty technical stuff, and you probably had no idea that marking tires could be so complicated. Well, it is. Anything worth doing is worth being complicated. We don't just blunder in there and start squirting tires. Some mutts do, but Drover and I are the elite forces of the Security Division, and we figure that anything worth doing . . . I've already said that.

I had just fought my way to Tire #2, when suddenly and all of a sudden, the door flew open and an angry man leaped out. See, some drivers resent dogs marking their tires. It makes 'em mad and sometimes they yell and screech and try to disrupt our mission. We have a response to this. We call it "Too Bad." We go right on with the mission and ignore their threats and noise.

No ordinary dog would dare to do that, but here at the ranch, we do it all the time.

Okay, this guy leaped out of the pickup and . . . hang on, this gets a little scary . . . and he didn't respond with the usual stuff—you know, the yelling and hissing and so forth. No sir. He did things I'd never seen before, things to which we hadn't been trained to respond. To. To respond to. Two "to"s.

Are you ready for this?

I'm not so sure you are. It's so shocking, you may want to think about it for a minute.

If you decide to skip over the scary part, that'll be okay. Go directly to Chapter Five and don't pause to look at Chapter Four. We'll regroup on the other side, see, and nobody will call you a . . . well, a weenie, for example, or any other tacky name. No name-calling here. Honest.

You be the judge.

Okay, I guess some of you are still with me. Thanks. This'll be pretty rough, and I'm glad to have your support in troubled times.

Here we go. This guy didn't just step out and

yell. He LEAPED out, made claws with his hands, made fangs with his teeth, and came RUNNING toward me! Oh, and he was also GROWLING! And he had a horrible ugly face. Horrible.

Honest. This is no exaggeration.

What kind of person would do such things? I had no idea. The man was obviously some kind of . . . I don't know what. A disturbed person, perhaps even . . .

We fed all our information straight into Data Control and got back a shocking message. It said that this guy had all the markings and so-forths of . . . you'd better hang on for this . . . *a vampire!*

CHAPTER FOUR

Holy Smokes, a Vampire on the Ranch!

D on't laugh. Vampires growl and bite and show their teeth, right? And they're ugly, right?

When an unauthorized vehicle pulls up in front of the house, we never know who or what it might contain. Maybe it's a family out for a Sunday drive in the country, but maybe it's not. Maybe it's a carload of . . . vampires or grave-robbers or escaped crinimals or . . . we never know.

We try not to think about such things. I mean, we have a job to do and we can't dwell on all the terrible things that could happen to us when we're making a Short Squirt Procedure.

And there I was. I had just moved into position

and was about to initiate the procedure on the rear tire, when this lunatic vampire came flying out the door, made claws, bared his teeth, started growling, and came lurching toward me.

I was frozen by fear. Never in my entire career had I seen anything quite like this. I saw the veins bulging in his horrible eyes. I even saw . . . or thought I saw . . . *blood* dripping off his fangs. In a flash, I threw all circuits over to Data Control's Master Program, and things started happening real fast. Right away, we got a warning light on the Coolant Panel. The cryogenic cooling system that ran the Squirt Program had just failed. We were getting nothing but tiny droplets through the system. All at once, the mission was on hold.

Then, seconds later, we got a second alarm, this one even more frightening than the first. Master Control had gone to Condition Red, and we had gotten the order to go to *Vampire Countermeasures*.

Perhaps you're surprised that we had trained for this contagency. We had. Even though the chances of finding vampires on the ranch were pretty low, we had prepared for it. Our training called for a rapid, multi-layered response. Would you like to take a peek at it? I don't suppose it would hurt.

First thing, we went to Full Flaps on the ears—

jumped 'em up to their very highest position. Next, we uttered a code word that locked in the Vamp-Count program. The code word, in case you'd like to know, was . . . "HUH?" That short, three-letter word kicked in Vampire Countermeasures and things started happening real fast.

We went to Full Reverse on all engines and began moving backward at a high rate of speed, but at the same time, we launched a bark that was intended to freeze the emeny in his tracks. The enemy, I should say, freeze the enemy in his tracks.

Well, it didn't work. He kept coming, slouching, growling, and making threatening gestures with his teeth, eyes, and claws. We launched a second bark, this one even bigger than the first. We had to do something to stop the guy, or at least slow his rate of attack.

He kept coming.

Well, by this time it had become crystal clear that this was no ordinary vampire. *He ate dogs*. And fellers, once our intelligence network had established this fact, we had pretty muchly run out of options. We had trained for Moderate Vampires, not Serious Vampires, and all at once our hands were cut out for us.

Up in the cockpit, I heard the voice of Master Control: "Uh, Lone Ranger, we're showing a Condi-

tion Dark Red. We need to get you out of there right away. We're switching you over to the Sell-the-Farm Program. Take cover, and good luck, soldier."

There you are. You heard it from the voice of Master Control, just as I did, and no doubt you shared with me the tension and seriousness of the moment. Pretty scary, huh? You bet it was, but I tried to warn you.

Are you still with me? Hang on. We're not out of the woods yet.

Okay, let's back up for a second. Master Control broke in on our normal communications channel and told us to switch to the Sell-the-Farm Program, right? This was a deeply coded message and you're probably wondering what it meant. That's the whole purpose of codes, see, to confuse the enemy.

Maybe you knew that.

In our code system (we were using the Ultra Confuso code that month), we didn't use such battle terms as run, Mayday, retreat, or help. Those were common words, and they were known to our enemies, so we had a heavily coded expression that meant the same thing: *Sell-the-Farm.*

Pretty clever, huh? Good thing I'm here to explain all this stuff.

Well, when my inner ears picked up that coded

message, I prepared to eject and scuttle the ship—or, to keep within the perambulates of the coding system, to "Sell the Farm." Things happened very fast. I abandoned the Marking Procedure and blew out of there in a cloud of dust, leaving the savage vampire to wonder how I had managed to escape the clutches of his clutch.

Here's how I did it. You'll be impressed, I think. See, instead of running far away, as most ordinary dogs would have done, I *pretended* to run far away and wiggled myself beneath the vampire's pickup—the very last place a vampire would look for his victim.

Awesome, huh?

And once hidden in the basement of his pickup, I assumed the Stealthy Crouch Position, which means that I neither moved nor breathed nor nothinged, and therefore became invisible to Vampire Vision and even enemy radar.

There . . . I waited. The silence, the tension, the pressure were almost unbearable. My ears picked up the sound of footsteps, yet I remained in the Frozen Stealth Position. I dared not move. Then, out of the corner of my periphery, I saw . . .

HUH?

. . . a face. A human face. A grinning human . . .

Okay, relax. This was just a, uh, test of our . . .

We've discussed Slim Chance, right? And his twisted infantile sense of humor? He thinks he's some kind of comedian and he seems to get weird pleasure out of making ME the butt of his laughingstock.

If it happened only once or twice a year, I could overlook it, but it happens over and over and again and again. Sometimes I even get the feeling that... well, he doesn't take my job very seriously. I'm sorry to put it that way, but the evidence derned sure points in that direction.

Here's the deal. There was no vampire. Slim was the driver of the pickup all along, and let me hasten to add that he'd done something to disguise his pickup. He'd... I don't know what he'd done, but it looked different, very different. Maybe he'd washed off some of the caliche dust. Yes, that was it, and when he saw me rushing to mark his tires—*taking care of ranch business*—when he so-forthed me so-forthing the pickup, he just couldn't resist indulging himself in childish follyrot, and he did that vampire routine.

Oh sure, I'd seen it all before. He'd pulled it on me a dozen times. It was an old, tired, stale joke—only this time he gave it a new twist. Always before, see, he'd done Vampire with his own natural face, but this time he just happened to be in possession of Little Alfred's Halloween mask, which was the face of a . . . something.

Okay, maybe it was a gorilla mask, but in the heat of battle, who the heck knows a gorilla from a vampire? And who has time to sit there and figure it out?

Any dog who saw that face would have thought it was a vampire. I mean, he was making claws and growling, don't forget that, and slouching toward me like . . . I don't know what. Like some kind of huge Frankincense Monster, and any Head of Ranch Security would have . . .

Well, our eyes met. He was grinning, obviously very proud of himself—for *what* I couldn't imagine. I, on the other hand, beamed him Looks of Wounded Pride, and went to Slow Taps on my tail. Tap, tap, tap. Through looks and taps, I sent him a message:

"I can't believe you've done this to me again. I can't believe I fell for it again. It saddens me that you would make such a mockery of my position on this ranch."

He got a huge chuckle out of it, of course, and to add to the sadness of the occasion, Little Alfred peeked under the pickup and saw me in my state of . . .

I held my head at a proud angle and tried to salvage a few shreds of dignity. Throughout the ages, small minds have always scoffed and giggled at the bold and the brave—at anyone who dared to be different or to think new thoughts.

Sir Figgly Newton invented the apple—and they laughed.

Galileo invented pizza—and they laughed.

Shakesbeer wrote tender poems—and they laughed.

Columbus discovered Ohio—and they laughed.

The names roll on and on—inventors, explorers, poemers, generals, heroes—and they were all mocked by the small minds of their day. Fine. I would take my place with those proud names and . . . phooey.

Slim thought he was so funny. Well, he wasn't funny, not at all, but never mind.

After he had gotten his yuks and giggles out of my misfortune, he tried to make peace with me.

"Did you think I was a gorilla monster, Hankie?"

No. I thought you were a childish nincompoop.

"Well, I just couldn't resist."

Yes, I was aware of that.

"Come on out and let's be pals again."

Pals? Ha! The damage had already been done. Sorry. Wounds just didn't heal overnight, and some wounds never healed at all.

"Oh, come on."

No. I had been shamed and humiliated. I had no choice but to remain under the pickup forever and ever. Slim could just find himself another dog.

"Hey, pooch, I found a stray dog wandering around on the county road. You might want to come out and meet him."

HUH?

A stray dog? On my ranch? Why hadn't I been informed . . .

Okay, it appeared that we had a stray dog situation on the ranch. Duty was calling. I swallowed my wounded pride and wiggled myself out from under the pickup.

That's when I met Jake.

Jake, the
Strange Bird Dog

Everyone on the ranch came out to see this new dog: Sally May, Baby Molly, Alfred, Pete, and even Loper. Loper had been working on the tractor and must have heard Slim's pickup approaching.

How did I know that Loper had been working on the tractor? Easy. He reeked of diesel fuel, and he had smudges of grease on his hands, clothes, and left cheek. The cowboys on this outfit aren't very good at mechanic work, see, and they always end up wearing dease and griesel.

Grease and diesel, shall we say.

Oh, and he was in a foul mood. They're always mad when they have to work on machinery.

He was wiping his hands on a red grease rag. His eyes went to me, and then to Slim. "What was Hank doing under your pickup?"

Slim chuckled. "We was playing Monster Watch, and I think I had him pretty well fooled."

He held up the gorilla mask. Loper scowled at it and wagged his head back and forth. "Well, we don't get much work done on this ranch, but we keep the dogs entertained. That's important. And speaking of dogs, what's that in the back of your pickup?"

All eyes swung around to . . . the new dog. He appeared to be one of your varieties of bird dog—short hair, white with spots, floppy ears, and a long stick tail. He was old and skinny.

"I found him up on the county road. He's wearing a collar with the name 'Jake.' I reckon that's his name."

Loper walked closer to the pickup and looked down at Jake. "What did you have in mind for Jake?"

"Oh, let him camp with Hank and Drover 'til the owner shows up. Somebody'll be looking for him, don't you reckon? Maybe they was out hunting quail and Jake wandered off."

Loper reached out his hand and rubbed Jake on the head. Jake looked away. "He's not very friendly, is he?"

"Well, that's a bird dog for you. They spend all their time in a kennel and it kindly warps their brains. I've got the same problem, only mine comes from being stuck out here on this workhouse of a ranch. Never get a day off. Never get to go to town. Never have any fun."

Loper stared at him. "Well, you and Jake ought to be great pals, you're so much alike. Why don't you haul him down to your place?"

"'Cause there's no dogs down there and he'd run off."

"Tie him up."

"Then he'd moan and cry all night and I'd miss my beauty sleep."

"I'd say that you've already missed most of it."

"Yeah, but if I missed any more, I wouldn't be as sweet and charming as usual, and then we'd have a grouchy hired hand trying to get along with a grumpy boss. Oh, by the way, I ran into Deputy Kile on the road. He says there's a saddle thief in the county."

"A saddle thief! We haven't had one of those in a long time."

"Yalp. We'd better keep an eye out for strangers."

Loper shook his head and looked away. "Okay, unload the dog. But if the owner doesn't show up in a few days, we're going to move him down to your place, since this was your big idea. Three days, that's it."

Slim let down the tailgate of the pickup and called Jake. Jake ignored him, and even turned the other direction. Slim grumbled and ended up having to drag the dog to the rear of the pickup and set him on the ground. Then he called me over to meet the new dog.

Have we discussed my position on bird dogs? I don't like 'em, never have. In the first place, they all seem to be a little weird. I mean, chasing birds is a pretty strange thing for a dog to do, isn't it? And in the second place . . .

It hurts me to say this, but we might as well go straight to the truth. *A bird dog stole the lady of my dreams.*

There. Now it's out on the table. We're talking about Miss Beulah the Collie, of course, and her pal Plato. Ah, sweet Beulah of the flaxen hair and the long collie nose! Be still my heart! I could never understand what she saw in that mutt, or why she would chose a bird dog over a cowdog, but she did. I'll say no more about it.

Yes, I will. It broke my heart into thirty-seven pieces and I may never get over it. When they put up my tombstone, I want it to say in big letters, "WHAT DID SHE SEE IN THAT CREEP?"

I try to go on with my life, but it's not easy.

I still dream about her, and one of these days . . . oh well.

But the point is that I don't like bird dogs, never have, and never will, and when Slim called me over to meet his new bird dog pal, I went—but only because it was forced upon me.

"Hankie, this here's Jake. Y'all are going to be good buddies for a few days."

I looked at Jake and he . . . gave me a glimpse and then looked away. The guy had no manners at all. This wasn't going to work, I could see that right away, and to express my feelings on the subject, I raised a strip of hair along my backbone and gave him a curled lip and a growl.

Slim nudged me with his boot. "Hey. None of that. Get along with him and keep him out of trouble. That's your job, pooch."

My job? Hey, I already had a job. In case he hadn't noticed, I was Head of Ranch Security, which had nothing to do with baby-sitting stray bird dogs or playing foolish monster games with idle cowboys.

Slim was still looking at me. "Hank, I'd be pleased if you volunteered for this job."

Volunteered? Me? Ha. He could forget that.

"'Cause if you don't volunteer, I'll be forced to yoke you and Jake together with a short piece of rope, so's y'all can get acquainted."

What? He wouldn't dare.

I didn't think he would yoke us together, but derned if he didn't. Next thing I knew, he'd tied us together, collar to collar, with a three-foot piece of hay twine.

"Now, when y'all decide to be nice and get along, I'll take off the twine. 'Bye now. I'll check you later."

He climbed into his pickup and drove down to the corrals. Loper went back up to the machine shed. Sally May, Baby Molly, and Alfred went to town for Alfred's dentist appointment.

Suddenly I found myself alone with this . . . this sour, skinny old bird dog. Our eyes met. His were kind of squinty, as though he couldn't see real well.

I was the first to make an effort to establish the friendship. I said, "I don't like bird dogs."

To which he replied, in a kind of mumbling, muttering voice, "I must get back to my work."

"That sounds good to me, pal. I have things to do myself. See you around."

Having established our relationship, we headed out of there in opposite . . . GULK . . . directions, only we were . . .

"Hey, I'm going west. I have to do a patrol of the corral area."

"I must return to Madagascar," he grumbled.

"Great. Go to Magadascar . . . Malagasper . . . go wherever you want."

And with that last exchange, we parted company. I headed west and the bird dog . . . GULK! Do you see what Slim had done to me? He had tied me to this . . . this sour, ill-tempered bag of bird dog bones, and . . . okay, I would just have to drag the mutt around with me. I had no other choice, because I had no intention of sitting there in front of the house all day.

I went west and the bird dog went south. I pulled and tugged. He pulled and tugged. Ten minutes later, we had drifted about twenty feet to the southwest, and we were both tired and out of breath.

We paused and glared at each other. At last I broke the icing. "Okay, pal, this isn't working. It seems that our destinies have been yokeled, and it's clear by now that we can't go in opposite directions. I guess we're going to have to discuss this."

"I must return to my work. They're waiting for me in Madagascar."

"Who's waiting for you?"

He glanced around. "I can't tell you."

"All right, then where's Magasaki?"

"*Madagascar.* I can't tell you."

"Well, that's just fine, birdbrain, because I

really don't care and didn't want to know in the first place. You go your way and I'll head for the corrals, and we'll just see who gets there first."

We parted company and the pulling match began again. Maybe you think I succeeded in dragging Jake all the way down to the pens. No. Dragging around forty pounds of bird dog bones isn't as easy as you might think. With our heads pointed at each other, we pulled and struggled, grunted and glared. Before I knew it, we had stumbled just far enough to the southwest to get ourselves wrapped around a chinaberry tree.

There, we came to a stop. Panting for our respective breaths, with our heads on opposite sides of the tree, we had reached a dead end.

"Okay, pal, let's go back to square one. Shall we introduce ourselves?"

"No. I don't like you."

"Well, you know what? I don't like you either. I disliked you on sight."

"You're keeping me from my work."

"And you're keeping me from mine. What should we do about that?"

"Go away. I want to be alone and quiet, with no one to bother me."

I managed a bitter laugh. "Hey, nothing would please me more than for you to be alone and quiet

and about fifty miles from here. Unfortunately, that's not where we are. We are high-centered on a tree, and until one of us moves, we're going to stay here. Do you want to stay here all day and all night?"

"No. I have work, important work."

"Then maybe we should talk, only it's hard to talk when our heads are on opposite sides of a tree trunk. If you will move three steps to the right, we'll be able to see each other."

"No. I'll not budge."

"Great, fine. You'll not budge, we'll not talk, and we'll just stay here until the buzzards come to clean up the mess."

Two hours passed. *Two hours!* I thought I would die of boredom. In sheer desperation, I came up with a compromise plan.

"Jake? Are you listening?"

"No."

"Yes you are, so listen some more. I've come up with a plan. If you move three steps to the right and if I move three steps to the left, we'll get unhooked from this tree. Moving to the left or right isn't the same as backing down. Do you follow me?"

"No. I want to be alone."

"Move three steps!"

There was a moment of throbbing silence. Then . . . "All right. Three steps, not one step more."

After a few failed attempts, we both moved three steps and managed to disengaged ourselves from the stupid tree. We glared at each other. Since we'd already wasted enough time tied to the tree, I broke the silence.

CHAPTER SIX

The Drama Gathers Momentumum

"All right, now we can talk. Point One: this is all your fault. You're the one who wandered away from your quail hunt and got lost."

"They left me no choice. I had to get back to Madagascar."

"Yeah? Well, I don't know where Madagascar is, but I think you missed it by a couple of miles, and here you are, ruining my life. I hope you're happy."

"I'm not happy. I want to be alone."

I rolled my eyes. "You still don't get it. We're tied together. You can't be alone. Even worse, I can't be alone. Slim did this because . . . I don't know why, but the point is, Jake, and I want you to listen very closely to this . . . the point is that we have to *work together* on this deal. Do you understand?"

I looked into his eyes. They were . . . distant. Empty. How do you communicate with a guy who doesn't even look at you? I didn't know, but I had to try.

"Okay, you leave me no choice. You've forced my hand and now I have to . . . well, use manners." Boy, that hurt. I took a deep breath and plunged into it. "Jake, my name is Hank the Cowdog. I'm Head of Ranch Security, and you might say that I own this outfit. Speaking on behalf of the Security Division and the entire staff, I'd like to welcome you to the ranch. We hope your stay with us will be a pleasant, happy, fulfilling experience."

Speaking such lies and rubbish almost killed me. But you know what? It seemed to help. For the first time, he looked me in the eyes. Then he glanced over his shoulders and whispered, "Who sent you?"

"Well . . . uh . . . I don't know. Slim, I guess."

"Did *they* send you or did you come on your own? I have to know."

"Tell me more about who *they* are?"

Again, he looked over his shoulders. "The pirates. They've taken Madagascar."

"No kidding."

"Yes. I've heard it. It must be true."

"Well, darn. Uh . . . this Madagascar . . . I guess

it's a town in the Texas Panhandle, huh?"

He beamed me a glare. "No, you fool, it's an island."

"Oh, sure, right. I remember now. It's an island off the coast of . . . it's down by Muleshoe, right?"

"No. Off the coast of Africa."

"Okay, now we're cooking. That's down by Lubbock, and you say these, uh, pirates have captured it, huh?"

"Yes. And unless they're stopped, they will find . . ." He leaned forward and dropped his voice to a whisper. ". . . the treasure!"

"No kidding. The treasure, huh?"

"Shhhhh! Not a word, not a word to anyone. This must be kept secret."

"Oh, sure, but you don't need to worry about me blabbing things around. I'm in the Security Business, don't you know, and we keep secrets all the time."

"Good. It mustn't leave this room."

Room? I glanced around and saw a tree, several birds, and a lot of buffalo grass. This guy was definitely a little strange. "Okay, so where are we with this deal?"

Jake cut his eyes from side to side. "I must return to Madagascar at once. Otherwise, the treasure will be lost."

"Good point. Now Jake, listen to me. I want you to go to Magdalena."

"Madagascar."

"Whatever. And I might be able to help you, but first we have to get unhitched."

"Ah. You mean the rope?"

"Yes, I mean the rope—only it's baling twine, not rope."

"I don't care."

"Good, neither do I, so let's mush on. Slim won't untie us until he sees us walking around together and thinks we've become pals."

"Ah. Do you have a plan for this?"

"Sure. He's working down at the corrals. If we can figure out how to walk down there together, maybe he'll cut us loose."

"It might work."

"Of course it'll work. Then you can take off for Magnacarta."

"Madagascar."

"Look, buddy, I'm having a little trouble with the name. Don't get your nose out of joint."

He stared at me with those veiled eyes. "There's nothing wrong with my nose. I have a brilliant nose. I've won many shows. I was offered a position as Professor of Quail."

"Yeah, and my name's Lulu."

"What?"

"Nothing. Let's try to walk down to the corrals."

It wasn't as easy as you might suppose, walking together as a team. I did my part, but every once in a while, Doctor Dingbat would start wandering off and we would get ourselves into another tug of war. The guy had no common sense. None. Zero.

Professor of Quail. What a joke.

It took him a while to get the pattern down, but at last he figured out that if we walked side by side, the deal would work, and by the time we reached the corrals, everything was hunky-dory. A careless observer might have thought we'd become the best of pals.

Ha. I couldn't wait to get rid of the pest. The sooner he left for Melagasper, the better I'd like it.

Slim was in the wire lot, ground-training a colt. He was walking behind the colt, driving him with something called "lunch lines" and teaching him to gitty up and whoa. Horses are such dumbbells, they have to be taught the very simplest of commands.

I mean, think about it. If you're a horse, a working professional ranch horse, you don't have to speak Greek and Hebrew. All you have to know is two words: gitty up and whoa. But do you suppose they come into this world prepared for their job? Heck no. They have to be coached and taught and trained, fussed over and mollycoddled, just so they can learn two words.

A dog would be fired for such incompetence.

They are pure dummies, but of course they don't know it. They are vain, cocky, arrogant, and overbearing, and worst of all, they will *chase dogs*. Yes. They will chase dogs, bite dogs with their big, green-stained teeth, and will even kick dogs for no reason at all.

Okay, maybe we bark at them sometimes, but that's no reason . . . never mind. I don't like 'em, that's the point.

So Slim was wasting his time, trying to teach a couple of simple words to a lead-brained colt, and he saw us walking up to the corral. He stopped his work and came over to the corral fence. He looked down at us and nodded his head.

"This is looking better. I guess you boys figured out how to get along."

I gave him Sincere Wags and Earnest Ears, as if to say, "Oh yes, Jake and I have become dear friends, the very best of friends. Ours is a friendship that will last a lifetime . . . or at least a couple of days. Now, could we, uh, do something with the twine?"

He gave it some thought. "Okay, I'll cut y'all loose. But Hank, I won't stand for any fighting, and I want you to stick close to old Jake. I have a feeling that he ain't playing with a full deck of cards."

I stared at him in disbelief. He was telling ME that? Oh brother! As if I didn't already know.

He cracked a smile. "See, one of us has to keep an eye on him, me or you, and since I'm a senior

executive around here, I decided to let you volunteer. Besides, I've gotta go feed the cattle in the middle pasture."

Very funny. He was too lazy to take care of his own messes, but that was okay. I've always known that, in many ways, this is a lousy job, but I could put up with Jake for a couple of days. I would do the job of a loyal dog, put in my time, and look forward to the moment when we could put wheels under Jake and send him down the road.

But the impoitant port is that Slim cut the twine, and at least I was no longer tied to the old crowbait. Important point.

When Jake realized that we'd been separated, he glanced around and whispered, "Ah. The way is clear. I must leave for Madagascar at once." And he started walking away.

I ran and caught up with him. "I'm supposed to stick with you, pal, and help keep you from doing something stupid."

"I don't need any help."

"That's a matter of opinion, I guess. How do you plan to get to this place?"

Once again, he gave me that secret look. "You won't tell?"

"Promise."

"There's a secret passage."

"A secret passage on my ranch? Ha, ha. Jake, if there were a secret passage on this outfit, I would have found it long ago."

"I'll show you . . . but you must tell *no one*."

I rolled my eyes. "Okay, buddy, show me the secret passage. We've got nothing better to do for the next three days."

I followed him up to the area just west of the house. Loper was welding inside the machine shed, and the glow from the welder cast eerie shadows across the gravel drive. Jake saw this and stopped.

He glanced around and whispered, "It's the Northern Lights. We were blown off course in a storm. This must be Iceland."

"It's a welder, Jake, and we're in Ochiltree County."

"You don't know them as well as I. They'll stop at nothing to keep me away from the treasure. You have much to learn."

He headed west in a long trot, toward an old shed that sat just west of the chicken house. I was about to follow, when Loper came out of the machine shed. He looked mad.

"The only thing worse than welding on busted farm equipment is running out of welding rods in the middle of a job. Now I have to make a trip to town."

He stormed over to his pickup and drove away.

Maybe you don't see the significance of this. At the time, neither did I, but it turned out to be a very important clue in the unfolding drama. Here, check this out.

Clue #1: Sally May, Baby Molly, and Alfred had left the ranch thirty minutes ago.

Clue #2: Loper had just left to get welding rod.

Clue #3: Shortly after Loper went to town, Slim finished working with the colt and went off to feed cattle.

Do you see the pattern developing? Don't forget that Slim had said something about a saddle thief. You'd better hang on. The scary part is coming.

The Mysterious Visitor

Okay, where were we? Oh yes, everyone had left the ranch, and I had to run to catch up with Jake the Uninvited Bird Dog. When I caught up with him, he was standing in front of the old shed, and he appeared to be muttering to himself.

"This could be it. Yes, I'm sure it is."

I glanced around and saw nothing that seemed unusual or important. "What are you looking at?"

His head whirled around. "Shhh! Do you want to give away my plans?"

"Plans for what? What are you doing?"

He lifted his eyes to the sky and heaved a sigh. "How can I do my work . . . *this is the entrance to the secret passage, you noodle!*"

I looked it over. "No, Jake, I think you're the

noodle in this haystack. That happens to be the entrance to the underside of the shed. There's nothing under there but dirt and a cinderblock foundation."

He gave me a sneer. "What do you know? Have you ever traveled the world, been to the Seven Seas, stood on the coast of Madagascar?"

"Well, I . . . no."

"Then please be silent." He glanced around. "I'm going. You may come or not, it's of no matter to me."

"No thanks."

"So be it. To Madagascar!"

He dropped down on his belly and began wiggling into the narrow space between the shed and the ground. Soon only his stick tail was showing, and then even that vanished. I stuck my nose into the dark space and looked into the gloom.

"Hey, is there really a secret passage in there?"

"Of course there is. Are you coming?"

Well . . . hmm. On the one hand, I wasn't too fond of dark narrow spaces, but on the other hand . . . gee, what if there really was a secret passage? That was the kind of information a dog should know about his own ranch, and what the heck, a short trip to Magabaster might be kind of . . . well, fun.

Don't get me wrong. I wasn't the kind of dog who was driven by a foolish desire to have fun all the time, but a little fun every now and then . . . don't forget the wise old saying: "All work and no play make Jack Sprat eat no fat." Is that what I wanted out of life? A life without steak fat or fatty ends of bacon? Heck no.

I mean, these wise old sayings have been passed down through the ages for a reason—to guide us and help us make difficult decisions— and it seemed pretty clear that I needed to spend a couple of hours sunning on the beaches of . . . whatever the name was.

So I plopped down on the ground and was about to embark on a new adventure, when all at once, my ears picked up a sound. Several sounds. Squeaking, rattling, and the hum of a motor. It appeared that we had a vehicle approaching head-quarters.

Slim, no doubt. Perhaps he had forgotten something. Or maybe he was coming back to play another silly, childish prank on me. Yes, of course. That fit Slim's pattern. If a joke works once, do it again and again, until you run it into the ground.

Ha. Well, he could play his pranks on someone else. Me? I'd been to school on pranks, and I wasn't about to . . .

All at once, Drover came running up. He had a worried look. "Hank, there's a pickup coming. Should we bark it up the drive?"

I greeted him with a glare. "Drover, I'm well aware that a pickup is coming. I'm also well aware that it's probably Slim. I recognize the rattles of his pickup."

"I'll be derned. It didn't look like Slim's pickup to me."

"Did you trouble yourself to take a closer look? Why don't you go check the tires for Secret Encoding Fluid?"

"Well . . . that seems like a lot of trouble."

"I see. You're too lazy and shiftless to check it out, and now you expect me to run up to the road and do your work for you. Is that what you're saying?"

He looked up at the clouds. "Well . . . I wouldn't have put it that way. See, I've been kind of busy."

"Doing what? Oh, and by the way, I noticed that you vanished about three hours ago."

"Oh yeah, boy, what a scare. See, this pickup drove up to headquarters and a monster jumped out, terrible monster, and he tried to eat me so I thought I'd better hide in the machine shed."

Our eyes met. "Drover, I was there. I saw the so-called monster. It was Slim, wearing a gorilla mask. He was playing childish games."

"Aw heck. He sure fooled me."

"Exactly my point. He fooled you, Drover, so now you've come to bother me with . . ." By then, my ears had shifted into the Higher Alert Position, and they were picking up some odd sounds. "Hmm. Drover, this new vehicle doesn't sound exactly like Slim's pickup."

"Yeah, it has a different set of squeaks."

I glared at the runt. "Are you explaining this case or am I?"

"Well . . ."

"I was about to say, before you butted into my lecture, I was about to say that this new vehicle has a different set of squeaks."

"I'll be derned."

"Which leaves open the possibility . . ." I began pacing, as I often do when my mind is racing at a high rate of speed. "Drover, I don't want to alarm you, but we must consider the possibility that *this vehicle is not Slim's pickup.*"

"That's what I said. I think that's what I said."

"Different squeaks mean a different pickup, Drover. Don't you get it? Slim doesn't drive a different pickup. He drives one that's always the same. Holy smokes, we may have blown the case wide open." I stopped pacing and whirled around. "Do you see where this is leading?"

"Well . . . not really. No."

I cut my eyes from side to side and dropped my voice to a whisper. "The saddle thief, Drover. Remember what Slim said about the saddle thief? This could be him! Everyone is gone, Drover, and we are now the ranch's only line of defense. Are you ready for some serious combat?"

His eyes crossed. "What's under the shed?"

"What? Oh, the shed. A secret passageway to some island, but that has nothing to do with this case. Are you ready for some serious . . ."

In a flash, he was gone. Before my very eyes, he zipped under the shed.

"Drover, come out this very instant, and that is a direct order!"

I heard his voice. "Hank, there's a bird dog in here."

"That's Jake, but he's already gone to Mega-blaster, so it couldn't possibly be him."

"I think I'll go with him. This old leg just went out. It's killing me!"

"Drover, come out here. We have a very important mission."

"Oh, my leg!"

My gaze darted from side to side. Did I dare take the time to deal with Drover's disobedience and give him the tongue-lashing he so richly deserved? My ears caught the sounds of the pickup. It had just pulled up in front of the corrals.

"Drover, this could be a very dangerous assignment. I'm sure you wouldn't want me to handle it alone . . . would you?"

"Oh heck no."

"Good. Come out at once. As the elite troops of the Security Division we'll go down and check it out together."

"Boy, that sounds great. I always wanted to be a leaky troop."

"Good. Let's move out."

"You know, I'd love to go with you, but I'm on a desert island and the pirates are coming. Jake said so."

"Don't listen to Jake. Listen to me. Hello? Drover?"

"I can't hear you, Hank. We're surrounded by pirates and monkeys throwing coconuts! You'd better go on without me."

"Very well, Drover, I'll have to handle it myself, but I must warn you that this will all go into my report. I intend to throw the book at you."

"Oh darn."

"Two books. One for being a chicken liver, and the second for using naughty language in the line of duty."

"Oh drat."

"Three books! Keep it up, Drover, and you may even have to spend some time with your nose in the corner."

"The monkeys are coming!"

What were those two jugheads doing in there? Pirates . . . monkeys throwing coconuts . . . desert islands . . . Well, I didn't have time to deal with their problems. I had a problem of my own, and there was some chance that it might be a big one.

I swallowed hard and took a big gulp of air. I would have to go into this without a backup. I began creeping down the hill toward the corrals. Fifty yards from Point Zero, I paused to reconnoodle the situation. I lifted my ears to their Full Gathering Mode and squinted my eyes to . . . I don't know why I squinted my eyes, but it seemed to improve my vision.

Peering through a clump of dead weeds, I saw . . .

Are you ready for this? Hang on to something.

I saw a pickup that was NOT Slim's. It was a totally different, unidentified, unauthorized vehicle with a camper on the back, and it was backed up to the . . . uh-oh. It was *backed up to the saddle shed.*

Do you see the pattern here? It was looking bad,

very bad. And it got worse, because just then, I saw a man climb out of the pickup. Do I dare describe him? He was a smallish man with beady little eyes and a stringy black mustache. He wore a baseball cap on his . . . well, on his head, of course, I mean, where else would you . . .

He was wearing a baseball cap on his head and a pair of sneakers on his feet. Obviously, he was no cowboy. He glanced around in all directions, opened the saddle house door, and went inside.

Gulp.

This was it. The pieces of the puddle . . . the pieces of the puzzle, I should say, had fallen together, and okay, maybe I was a little nervous. Who wouldn't have been nervous?

We had a dangerous crinimal prowling around in the saddle shed.

I was alone on the ranch.

I would have to place my life on the clothesline and engage this guy in a fight to the death.

We just didn't know whose death would come first—mine or his.

Gee, What
a Nice Guy!

I went creeping toward the saddle shed door. At this point in the procedure, I still had a faint hope that this might turn out to be a false alarm.

I heard someone moving around inside. I lifted my right ear and fine-tuned the sound.

Sneakers, probably an older pair, moving about on the cement floor.

Okay, I was more than a little nervous, but who wouldn't have been? Think about it. There was only one way in and one way out of the saddle shed. Once I broke down the door and went charging inside . . .

HUH?

The door swung open and I saw the man come out.

It wasn't Slim. It wasn't Loper. *It was a man I had never seen before!*

Oh, and did I mention that he was carrying a saddle? Yes, he was carrying a saddle and he threw it into the camper and went back inside the saddle shed.

That could mean only one thing: HE WAS THE SADDLE THIEF!

Was I scared? Might as well come clean and admit it. Yes, I was scared, and we're not talking about mere nervousness or excitement or anticipation here. We're talking about plain old scared. And why not? I'd never tried to make a single-handed solo arrest of a saddle burglar.

Yes, my mouth was suddenly dry and my knees were suddenly feeling weak and trembly. I even threw a glance back over my shoulder, in the faint hope that Drover might have changed his mind and vultured out to help me. Ventured out, I should say. But that was a pretty faint and desperate hope, and it should give you some idea of how . . . well, small and lonesome I suddenly felt.

Gulk.

You know, sometimes a dog finds himself trapped by his own reputation, his own notion of who he is. Drover was still hiding under the tool-shed, but nobody expected anything else out of the runt. But with me . . . the expectations were high, including my own, and . . . gulp . . . that's what kept me moving forward, when certain parts of my body and mind would have sure preferred being somewhere else.

I took a deep breath of air and tried to calm my nerves. It would all be over in five minutes, and at that time it would either be a memory or . . . I didn't want to peek into that dark hole.

This was my job. It had to be done, and there was nobody else to do it.

I slipped up to the door and stepped inside. There he stood near the northwest corner. He was lifting a saddle off the saddle rack.

I saw no sign of a gun, knife, club, or bomb on his person. That was fairly encouraging news.

Could I take him, one-on-one? I did a quick review of all the moves and throws and punches and biting maneuvers I had learned about Marshall Art.

It's funny, the things that pop into your mind in moments of great tension. I had no idea who Marshall Art was.

But that thought passed quickly. The moment of truth had arrived.

He hadn't seen or heard me. He had no idea that he was being observed or that I was blocking the only doorway out.

I lifted Lip Shields and exposed Tooth Daggers. A deep rumbling growl began in the lower part of my throat. I went to Full Raised Hackles.

I had thrown down the goblet. The next move was up to him.

The growl startled him. His head shot up and he turned his head around, very slowly. It was then that I discovered a secret message written on the front of his cap. It said . . . *Richardson Seeds*.

Did that have any deep dark meaning? No. It was just a cap.

Our eyes met and were welded together by the fires of fear and suspicion. And maybe even hatred. I didn't know this guy and he didn't know me, but we came from opposite sides of the law, and that made us enemies—enemies for the moment, enemies for life, enemies forever.

His eyes narrowed. He ran his tongue over his upper lip—and also through that stringy mustache of his. I've never had any use for stringy mustaches or for the kind of creeps who wear them.

And then, in the silence, with the two of us facing each other and pondering the deadly combat that would surely follow . . . he spoke.

I know you're probably sitting on the very edge of your chair, scared out of your wits. I understand that. I could hear my old heart pounding like a whole marching band of bass drums.

Pretty scared.

Real scared.

When he spoke, his voice broke the brittle silence like . . . I don't know what. Like a tray of glasses dropped on the floor. Like a brick thrown through a window.

He spoke and here's what he said. "Well now! What have we here? It's a puppy dog." He gave me a weak smile. I answered with a firm growl. "I'll bet you're the guard dog around here."

Right.

"You sure are bristled up, but you know what, doggie? I'll bet me and you could be friends." He grinned. I didn't. "What do you say about that?"

Not a chance.

"Oh, I know what's eating you. You probably think I don't belong in here."

Right. Exactly.

"Well, that's easy. See, I'm a cobbler. I fix saddles and stuff for all these ranchers and cowboys, and your master . . . you know him, don't you?"

Of course I knew him.

"He called me just the other day and asked if I could come out here to the ranch and pick up a bunch of saddles, take 'em to my shop in town, oil 'em up real good, fix the busted saddle strings, stitch the horns and cantles, and just give 'em a regular tune-up. Did you know that?"

No.

"I mean, you look like the kind of dog who would know just about everything that happens on his ranch. Maybe your master just didn't want to trouble you with a tiny detail like this."

Well, I . . . yes, maybe Loper had mentioned something about it, but . . .

He shrugged and kept smiling. "He might not be too proud if he knew you was trying to keep me from doing my job. See what I mean?"

I wasn't convinced.

"Yes, I'm just an old boy who works hard to make a living. I've got a serious heart condition, you know." His eyes grew distant and the smile faded from his lips. "The doctors say . . . I don't have much longer for this old world, maybe two years, maybe . . . not even that long."

Gosh.

"And me and the little woman have five little kids—the cutest, sweetest little children you ever saw, and you know, they'd just fall in love with a dog like you. I always wanted to get 'em a dog, but . . . never could afford it."

Gee whiz. That was kind of touching.

"The little woman, she works all day at the

Dairy Queen, then she comes home at night and irons shirts for fifty cents apiece. I have this little saddle business, when my health permits me to work, but we just barely get by. You know, my friend, it's a hard old world out there."

Yes, I . . . I knew that.

"Anyway, I didn't want to burden you with my troubles. It's a good life. I just take it one day at a time and hope that . . . well, when I'm gone, the Good Lord will look after those little children."

Gosh. The poor kids.

He reached two fingers into his shirt pocket and came out with . . . what was it? A roll of something. He peeled off some paper and popped a brownish object into his mouth. He chewed it up and noticed that I was watching.

"Candy. Chocolate candy. You want one?"

No thanks. I never took candy from strangers. And besides, eating candy on duty was against regulations. No thanks.

"It's pretty good stuff. Kind of hard to chew, but I love chocolate. It's the one little luxury I allow myself. Sure you don't want some?"

I was sure. No candy, period.

"Well, at least come over and smell it. You might accidentally like it, and you might even decide that I'm not such a bad guy. Come on."

No, I really . . . okay, one little sniff wouldn't hurt anything.

I eased toward his outstretched hand, but I was ready to spring into action if this turned out to be some kind of trick. I gave it a sniffing and . . . hmm, by George, it did smell pretty good, but as far as eating chocolates on the job, I really . . .

"Go on, pup, take it. Don't you deserve a piece of chocolate?"

Well . . . yes, sure, since he put it that way. Maybe I did deserve a, uh, small reward.

I took it from his hand and backed away, just in case.

He was right about it being hard to chew. Musht have been caramel or whapever you call thap schick shewy shtuff. It kind of gummmmmed up my tcheeth and I had a heck of a chime . . . but delicious? Yes sir, it was . . . glop, slunk, smork . . . a great piece of candy.

"That's pretty fine candy, ain't it?"

Oh yeah. Delicious.

"It sure would gum up a set of false teeth, wouldn't it?"

Right. You bet.

"'Scuse me just a second, pup, and I'll load this last saddle in my pickup. I'll be right back. Don't go away."

Fine. Sure.

He left with the saddle and I concentrated on . . . you know, that candy was kind of like a tough piece of meat. The longer you chewed it, the bigger it got. I was still working on it when he came back and started looking at the bridles hanging on the wall.

"Well, lookie here. What a pretty silver-mounted bit! And didn't your master tell me that the head-stall on this bit needed some fixing?"

Yeah . . . slurp, glop . . . he probably did. Those guys were always tearing something up.

He hung the bridle on his shoulder and picked out another one. Then he looked down at me.

"You ready for another piece?"

No, by George, that was great candy, but it was about to wear me out.

He brought the roll out of his pocket, peeled off another piece, and flipped it in my direction, and more or less on instinct, I . . . well, snagged it right out of the air.

He laughed. "Nice catch, pooch. I can see that you're a pretty high-class kind of dog."

It showed, huh? This guy was pretty . . . slorp, glop . . . sharp.

"I shouldn't be eating candy anyways, not with this kidney problem of mine."

Yes . . . gorp, slop . . . that was true.

"I just hope the doctors find a cure before it's too late."

I went to Slow and Caring Wags on the tail section and gave him my most sincere look of sincerity.

"Well, see you around, Shep. It's been great knowing you."

And with that, he climbed into his pickup and drove away.

CHAPTER NINE

I'm Trapped in Madagascar!

G ee, what a nice guy. Imagine me thinking that he was a saddle thief!

Actually, I'd never been convinced that he was a thief—not 100 percent. Okay, maybe my first impression had been . . . that is, he'd seemed a little slippery at first, but first impressions are often false and incorrect. Once we'd established a deeper relationship, well, it became obvious that this was a good, honest, hardworking man who was just trying to support his family.

Great guy. And the fact that he gave candy to dogs . . . well, that didn't hurt his reputation at all. I mean, what kind of person gave candy to dogs? Only the best, brightest, and most sincere. And it really made me sad to know that he had that terrible heart condition.

Or was it his kidneys? Something like that. Yes, we would all hope for a cure.

Poor guy. And poor kids!

Well, it had been a pretty exciting day, with a few ups and downs, but everything had turned out just right. I couldn't wait to tell Drover about all the adventures he had missed, so I left the empty saddle shed and hiked up the hill and went straight to the toolshed. I poked my nose under the crawl space.

"Drover, are you in there?"

"Well . . . I'm not sure. Where's the saddle thief?"

I couldn't help chuckling at his weird ideas. "There was no saddle thief, just as I suspected, and if you'll come out, I'll tell you the whole story."

There was a moment of silence. "Oh . . . maybe I'd better stay here in Madagascar."

"Drover, please don't embarrass me. You're *under the toolshed.* There is no such place as Maskabatter."

There was a moment of silence. "Well . . . it looks pretty real to me. Palm trees. The ocean. Oh, and lookie there. It's a ship, a big ship. You ought to come in and see it, Hank. It's nice."

I heaved a sigh. "Okay, I'll come look, but I must warn you, Drover, I don't believe any of this stuff."

I began wiggling myself into the narrow crawl space. It was dark in there, very dark. It was also a very tight squeeze. And dusty. I crawled through the dusty darkness. The light from the entrance began to fade. At last I reached my nincompoop assistant.

He was grinning. "Well, here we are. Can you smell the ocean breeze?" I sniffed the air and . . . hmm, maybe it did smell a bit like the ocean. "And see those palm trees over there?"

I squinted into the dark distance. "Oh yes. Is that where the monkeys stay?"

"Yep, that's the place. Pretty, isn't it?"

"Well, I . . . it's awfully dark, Drover."

"Yeah, 'cause we're below the equator, and the sun's lefthanded."

"What?"

"I said . . . let's see. I said . . . I think I said . . ."

"Never mind, skip it. We've got business to discuss."

I told him the story of the poor little cobbler and how I had helped him in his efforts to support his family. He was so moved, he broke into tears. Drover did, not the cobbler. The cobbler was gone, see, and . . . skip it.

Drover broke into tears. "Gosh, that's one of the saddest stories I ever heard! I hope his kidneys hold out until they find a cure."

"Yes, we can always hope, but it was his heart. He's got a heart condition."

"I thought you said kidneys."

"Whatever, but the point is that I ended my mission with a good deed. And Drover, when we can solve a case and help someone at the same time, well, it just doesn't get much better than that."

"Gosh, how sweet."

"Yes indeed." My eyes prowled the gloomy darkness. "Drover, are you sure you saw some monkeys?"

"Oh yeah, no doubt about it. They were in those palm trees right over there."

"Hmm, this is very strange. One more question. Did those monkeys remind you of anyone we know?"

"Well, let me think here. They reminded me . . . of *me*. Is that the right answer?"

It took me a moment to recover from the shock of this revelation. "Yes, Drover, it's exactly the right answer. That was a trick question, and I used it to test the accuracy of your story. It seems that you passed—much to my amazement."

"So now you believe in Madagascar?"

"Logic is our light in the darkness, Drover, and we must follow it wherever . . ." Just then, I heard a vehicle approaching headquarters. "Ah, some-one's coming. Back to work, son, our little vacation is over. Let's wiggle ourselves out of here and regroup at the . . . hmmm, I seem to be . . . it's pretty cramped in here, isn't it?"

"Not for me. I'll meet you outside."

He wiggled away and I found myself staring into Jake's empty eyes. He spoke. "I don't like you. I'm going away. It's too crowded in Madagascar. Good-bye."

He wiggled his way toward the entrance.

"Fine with me, bud, and now I'll just . . . hey, Jake, hold up a second. I seem to be having a little . . . hey, I'm not sure I can get out of here!"

"You're too fat," he said, and then he was gone.

"Oh yeah? Well, you're going to have a fat lip if you don't . . . Jake, we need to discuss this, no kidding. Drover? Drover! Get yourself back in here and . . . HELP!"

Just when it appeared that I had solved the case and everything was turning out right . . . *I found myself trapped on a remote desert island!* Too much candy, I suppose.

Pretty scary, huh? You bet it was. I mean, you know where I stand on the issue of tight and creepy places, right? I hate 'em. I tried to turn around. I couldn't move.

Just then, in the silence and darkness, I heard Drover's voice. "Oh my gosh, Hank, come quick. Slim just drove up and and you know what he found? All the saddles are missing from the saddle shed!"

"Well, of course they are. I've already told you that a nice little cobbler showed up and . . ."

"Yeah, but he wasn't a nice little cobbler. He was a nice little *thief*. Slim said so."

HUH?

I cut my eyes from side to side. My thoughts tumbled and swirled. The pieces of the puzzle began falling . . . apart. Holy smokes, I had been duped, used, tricked by that sneaky little . . .

"Okay, Drover, listen carefully. We have a problem here. I'm trapped in Madagascar and you must . . . Drover? Drover!"

The little . . . I couldn't believe it. He had just walked off and left me in there—trapped, buried, untombed, stranded, alone! He would pay for this.

It was then that the full seriousness of my situation came crashing down on me. Maybe you think I just lay there in the darkness, crying over this cruel turn of events. No sir. I hit the Panic Alarm and went to Robust Howling and Moaning, fellers, and we're talking about pulling out all the stops. I was so desperate, I howled a song about my plike. Plite. Plight. Whatever.

I'm Trapped in Madagascar

I'm trapped in Madagascar and marooned
    upon this isle.
And to my friends who left me here, I say,
    "Guys, thanks a pile."
They left me here to rot and to be broiled by
    the sun,
But only if the bugs don't eat me and pirates
    do not come.

I'm trapped in Madagascar, the ship has
    sailed and gone.
I saw her three masts disappear below
    the horizon.
I took the secret passage and I trusted
    Jake the Dope,
And now I fear I've really hung myself,
    and even brought the rope.

I'm trapped in Madagascar and my mind
    is growing numb.
What really hurts my feelings, though,
    is it was pretty dumb
To trust a dingbat bird dog and what
    Drover said I'd find.
Sometimes I think I'm not just deaf and
    dumb, but also pretty blind.

I'm trapped in Madagascar, but I know
    it isn't real.
This place is just a toolshed, right?
    A phony put-up deal.
I never should have listened to that pair of
    dingy mutts.
Uh-oh, I see some monkeys coming . . .
    and they're throwing coconuts!

I howled and moaned for what seemed hours. Maybe it was just a couple of minutes, but it was long enough to get some results.

Slim heard me in my moment of greatest need, and though it took him a while to climb the hill and locate the sounds of my distress, at last I heard his voice.

I couldn't see him, since I was pointed in the wrong direction, but I heard him say, "Hank, what in the cat hair are you doing under the shed?"

Shed? Well, I . . . it was hard to explain. I had been baby-sitting his dingbat bird dog and . . . well, I'd gotten this report about pirates and monkeys on a . . .

Suddenly the clues came together and I saw the whole picture. This wasn't a desert island and there were no monkeys in the palm trees. And do you know why? Because I was trapped under the toolshed, and palm trees don't grow under tool-sheds.

No palm trees, no monkeys. No monkeys, no Magadaster.

But there was more, much more. My mind was racing over the evidence that had suddenly fallen into place. It occurred to me that Jake had lured me under the shed and had arranged this whole scam as a way of distracting me from the case, which could mean only one thing: *Jake was in cahoots with the saddle thief!*

It made sense, didn't it? They both had mysteriously showed up on the same morning, right? And Jake had tried to distract me with all his blabbering about . . . wherever it was . . . an island off the coast of Muleshoe. And now I was trapped under the very shed where he had led me.

What a fool I'd been! Not only had I trusted the so-called cobbler with the fifteen sick children, but I had been duped by his bird dog assistant. Oh, what a lowly fate, to be duped by a bird dog!

"Hank, come on out and quit your moaning and groaning."

Huh? Oh, that was Slim. My mind returned to the present moment. Was he kidding? Hey, I was trapped! Did he think I was enjoying this?

At last he figured out that I was in a Crisis Situation. He trudged a few steps to the machine shed and came back with a high-lift jack. With much mumbling under his breath, he slipped it between two cinder blocks and jacked up the south side of the shed.

Good old Slim! What a pal. He had saved me from a terrible fate. I wiggled myself around and began crawling out to the light. Once in the open daylight, I shook the dirt off my coat and . . . uh . . . dared to look into Slim's . . .

He was standing with his hands on his hips, towering over me and shaking his head. "Some guard dog you turned out to be. A guy comes onto the ranch and starts loading up all our gear, and you crawl under the toolshed and hide."

No, wait, it wasn't what he thought. That is, I knew it looked bad but . . . see, I met this guy down at the . . . he tricked me, see, he told me terrible lies and forced me to eat . . . uh . . . chocolate candy, and . . .

Okay, I'd made a mistake, a big mistake, but not the one Slim thought I'd made. I didn't run away and hide. I never would have done that, honest. I'd just . . . oh boy . . . made friends with the . . .

It was too complicated, I couldn't explain it. I went to Mournful Eyes. I lowered my head and pulled my tail up between my legs. I couldn't have sunk any lower if I'd been a snake.

Slim shook his head. "Hank, I never thought you were a coward. I guess I was wrong."

And with that, he walked down to the house and called the sheriff, leaving me alone with my thoughts and guilt. Actually, I would have been glad to be alone at that moment, but guess who chose that very moment to appear.

The guy I least wanted to see.

My least favorite character on the ranch.

The world's biggest pest and pain in the neck.

Pete.

I heard his purring behind me, and turned to see him come sliding along the south side of the machine shed. His tail was stuck straight up in the air and he was rubbing on the big sliding door. Oh, and he was grinning.

"Mmmm. How's it going, Hankie? Having a bad day?"

I shot him an ice-pick glare. "I'm sure you've been eavesdropping, Kitty, so you probably know that this hasn't been a great day for me. I've been accused of terrible crimes I didn't commit."

"Well, darn. Is there anything I can do to help?"

"Sure. Tell Slim that he got it all wrong. I knew that creep was stealing saddles, and I even went down to work the case."

By this time, he had run out of things to rub on and had begun rubbing on my legs.

"Yes? And what happened?"

"Don't rub on my legs, you little weasel."

He batted his eyes and grinned. "I thought you liked it."

"I don't like it. I hate it. What happened? Well,

I was about to make an arrest and blow the case wide open, when . . ."

His eyes popped open. "Yes?"

The air hissed out of my lungs. "He forced me to . . . well, to eat chocolate candy. It caught me off guard. How can a dog bite the hand that feeds him candy? If he'd kicked me or started yelling, I would have . . . skip it. Never mind."

"Poor doggie! And now everybody's mad at you and thinks you're a coward. How sad. I think I'm going to cry."

Do you think the little sneak started crying? Do you think he really cared? Well, hang on and you'll soon find out.

CHAPTER TEN

The Sheriff Arrives

Ha! No sir, Pete didn't start crying. He started *laughing*. Right there in front of me, in my hour of greatest darkness, he went into a fit of laughing.

Okay, that did it. I'd had just about all I could stand from Pete. More than I could stand, actually. I leaped to my feet, went to Full Fangs and Menacing Growls and was about to give him the . . .

HUH?

A vehicle was approaching. Two vehicles. The first one was . . . gulp . . . Loper's pickup, and I already had a feeling that he wouldn't be in a great mood when he learned . . . oh boy, how did I ever get into this mess?

The second vehicle was a red car with a badge

or something on the door. It belonged to the Ochiltree County Sheriff's Department. Things were beginning to look . . . pretty serious.

I slipped down the hill and took up a position behind some chinaberry trees. I listened and watched.

Sheriff Hataway and Deputy Kile got out, shook hands with Slim and Loper, and began their investigation. For half an hour, they took notes and measurements and studied the tracks on the ground. Then they got in the car and drove away.

Oh. Deputy Kile found dog tracks in front of the saddle shed.

Mine.

I didn't need to be told that I was fired. I would fire myself, resign my position in total disgrace. It was the only decent and honorable thing left for me to do.

Loper went back into the house, and an eerie calm fell over the ranch. With my head and tail hanging as low as they could hang, I made the long, slow walk to the gas tanks.

I wanted to feel sorry for myself. I wanted to make excuses for everything that had happened. But I couldn't. I had made one mistake after another, and now I would have to pay for them.

Drover was there when I arrived, and so typical of the little mutt, he had his head burrowed under his gunnysack bed and his stub-tailed hiney pointing northward and skyward. On another occasion, I might have scolded him, but now I caught myself smiling.

I mean, he really was a funny little guy. He couldn't stand to hear people yelling, even though they were usually yelling at me, and so he escaped to his own little world beneath the gunnysack.

I would miss him. Even though he had come close to driving me nuts on many occasions, he'd been a true friend. Sort of.

I sat down on the edge of my bed. "You can come out now, Drover. Everyone has gone and I have something to tell you."

The sack rustled and I saw one of his eyes peering out. "Is it safe? Gosh, what was all the yelling about?"

"Oh . . . it was about me, Drover. I've failed my ranch, my friends, myself . . . everything that's dear to me. I made a mess of this case. I had it in the grisp of my grasp, and I blew it."

"Gosh, what happened?"

I told him the whole story. "And you know what hurts me most about this, Drover? I trusted that creep. He told me one whopper of a lie after another, and I believed him. I felt sorry for him!

A poor cobbler with a heart condition, trying to scratch out a living for his wife and five hungry children."

Drover came out from under the sack. "Well, I believed it too. I cried when you told me, it was so sad."

"Sure, it was sad, and it was all lies. Oh, and then there was Jake. I fell for his line too."

"Jake? You mean . . ."

"Yes, Drover, Jake was in it from the start. No doubt he's the thief's stooge. It was his job to play the part of a goofy bird dog."

Drover gasped. "You mean . . . he's really not a bird dog?"

"We can't be sure at this point, but I have a suspicion that he's just a mutt wearing a bird dog disguise. They're very clever, you know. It was his job to wander into headquarters and throw me off the trail. And you know what? He succeeded."

"Gosh, I thought he was kind of nice. He took me to Madagascar."

I stared at the runt. "Drover, he didn't take you to Madagascar. You were under the toolshed."

"No, we went to a desert island and the monkeys threw coconuts at us and we found the buried treasure." He gave me a silly grin. "It was fun."

"Oh yeah? Then where's the treasure?"

"Well, let me think here. Oh yeah, the pirates stole it."

"How do you know that? Did you actually see them? Facts, Drover, dig deep for the facts."

"Well, let me think here." He wadded up his face in a pose of deepest concentration. "No, I didn't see 'em. But Jake did."

I rolled my eyes. "Oh, great. Jake's in cahoots with the saddle thief, and you believed him?"

"Well . . ."

"Drover, sometimes I'm shocked by your gullarulity."

"What's that?"

"It means that you fell for the whole story. I'm sorry but there's no nicer way to put it. You fell for his . . ." I got up and walked a few paces away. "But I fell for it too."

"Oh good. I feel better now."

"Better? You should feel *worse*, a thousand times worse. This gang of thieves not only outfoxed you, but they have made fools of the entire Security Division." I paced back to where he was sitting. "I don't get it, Drover. I've spent my whole life learning to be tough and hard-boiled, but what got me in the end was a tender heart. Now I must resign."

A tear slid down his cheek. "Resign! You mean . . ."

"Yes, this is the end. A guy can make a few bone-head mistakes and still keep his pride, but this one . . . no. There's no going back. I want to leave before they haul me off."

Tears glistened in his eyes as he nodded his head. "Gosh, where will you go? And who'll take care of the ranch?"

"I don't know where I'll go, just start walking, I suppose. And you'll have to take over my duties and run the ranch yourself."

He darted his head back under the gunny-sack. "Don't say that, I can't stand to hear it! I don't want a steady job, my leg just can't take it and . . ."

Just then, our conversation was interrupted by the sound of an approaching vehicle. I looked around and saw Slim's pickup pulling up to the gas tanks. He got out and began filling the tank with gas. I was in no mood for company, but just to be sociable, I gave him a weak smile and went to Slow Thumps on my tail.

He tossed a glance in my direction and shook his head. "Well, pooch, you really done it this time. A ranch dog, a cowboy's dog, and you let that sorry little crook drive down there and walk away with all our saddles!"

The words stung, but there was no way I could

explain that I had tried to stop him. At least I had *intended* to try to . . . oh well.

"Pooch, do you have any idea how it feels to be a cowboy, and to be afoot? It's a terrible feeling. And you know what else? To replace that saddle with one just as good would take a thousand bucks. And last time I checked, I had thirty dollars to my name. It makes me sick, and if I ever get my hands on that . . ."

He'd gotten so carried away with lecturing me that he'd forgotten about the gas he was pumping into his tank. All at once it was full and some of the gas shot out and sprayed his hand.

"DAD-gum gas! Now I've done it. When am I going to learn to pay a-dadgum-'tention?"

He hung the nozzle on its baling wire hook. I knew what was coming next, but instead of slinking away, as I had done in happier times, I went to him and offered myself as a grease rag. He seemed a little surprised.

He wiped his hands on my back and then scrubbed his fingernails on my ears. "Thanks, pooch." Then he smelled his hands. "Good honk, I'm not sure I done myself much good on that effort. You may smell worse than gasoline." He took my head in his hands and looked into my eyes. "How do you get yourself into so much trouble, Hank?"

I didn't even try to answer. It was too complicated. Jake. The phony little cobbler. The bogus
trip to Mogadishu.

"You're dumb. You was born dumb and you've
spent your whole life gettin' dumber." For a long
throbbing moment, we stared into each other's
eyes. "And you know what else? I've got the same
problem, like spraying myself with gas. I never
learn. I do it every cotton-pickin' time I fill up."

He straightened up and rolled a kink in his
back, adjusted his hat and looked up at the sky.
Then his gaze came back to me. I thumped my
tail.

"You feel pretty bad, don't you?" Yes, I did. "It
sure hurts when you mess up, don't it?" Yes, it
did. "Tell you what let's do, pup. You stay down at
my place for a couple of days. The scarcer you are
around here, the better it'll be for everyone, espe-
cially you. Come on, let's load up."

Well . . . sure, okay, why not? I didn't have any
better offers. I ran to the pickup door and waited
for him to open it. He came up behind me, shaking his head.

"Uh-uh. I'll try to forgive your many sins, bozo,
but I can't hack your smell in the cab. You ride in
the back."

Sure, fine, no problem there. Actually, I had

always preferred riding in the back, but I was just trying to be, uh, sociable.

I leaped into the back—and by the way, he didn't even have to let down the tailgate. I was so happy to have a friend and a place to go, I just flew over that rascal. As we pulled away, Drover crept out from under his gunnysack and waved good-bye.

"Are they going to hang you?"

"Not this time, Drover. I think we've worked something out."

"Oh good, I'm so happy."

"I'm going into exile for a couple of days."

"Boy, I love eggs. Hurry back."

I waved good-bye and off we went. At that point I sat down and prepared to enjoy the . . .

HUH?

I found myself staring right into the eyes of . . . someone. You'll never guess who or whom it was.

CHAPTER ELEVEN

I Pry a Confession out of Jake— the Wrong One

Give up? I knew you'd never guess.
It was Jake.

He was curled up in a ball of hair and bird dog bones, but he wasn't asleep. His eyes were open, and he was looking at me.

Maybe he knew what was coming. Maybe he saw my entire mouth turn into a wall of fangs, and maybe he heard the growl of righteous rumbling in my throat.

He said—and this is an exact quote—he said, "Don't strike me. I'm old and decrepit."

"Oh yeah? Well, you're fixing to be worse than that. I ought to tear you limb from tree."

"I want to be alone and quiet, with no one to bother me."

"Hey, I've heard that before, bud, only this time it won't cut bait. Jake, you're under arrest."

"I've done nothing. I'm an innocent dog."

I towered over him. "You're under arrest, and I think you know why."

He studied me with narrowed eyes. "All right. I did it. I'm glad I did it. I'll always be glad I did it. Nothing you can do will change me."

"Jake, I just don't understand creeps like you. How could you stoop so low?"

"I have nothing more to say."

"Slim picked you up on the road and gave you a place to stay. He trusted you. I trusted you. We opened our home to you, and then you used our kindness against us."

"Yes, and I would do it again."

"You ought to be ashamed."

"I am not ashamed."

I stuck my nose right in his bird dog face. "How could you not be ashamed? What kind of low-life creep are you?"

"The treasure was mine. I merely took it back."

I stared at him. "What are you talking about? You mean the saddles?"

"The treasure, you fool! The buried treasure on

the coast of Madagascar!" He glanced around, as though someone might be listening. "We found the treasure, on the beach, just where I had left it. The pirates came. Then we were attacked by monkeys."

"Throwing coconuts?"

"Who told you? I demand to know!"

I walked a few steps away to clear my head. "Jake, let me ask you one small simple question. Were you involved in a plot to steal saddles from our ranch? Were you working with a little guy with a stringy mustache?"

"Saddles? Ha! What would a bird dog do with a saddle?"

"I don't know. Answer the question."

"I know nothing about saddles. I know that the treasure is mine, all mine—diamonds, pearls, emeralds, rubies, gold, and silver. Your friend Drover thinks the pirates took it, but, ha ha, they did not. I led them to an empty chest and the fools took it. And now I am . . . rich."

The air hissed out of my body. "You're a lunatic."

"I am rich, and soon I will become the Emperor of Madagascar."

"You are so full of baloney, I can't believe it."

"Yes. And now I must leave. They are waiting for my return. Good-bye."

And then, before my very eyes, he crawled

beneath a canvas tarp, until only the tip of his long stick tail was showing. I knocked on the tarp.

"Hey. Where are you now?"

"The coast of Spain. Tomorrow, we sail with the tide. Leave me alone. Good-bye."

Well, so much for my case against Jake. For a while there, I had thought . . .

Actually, I had suspected all along that he . . . to tell you the truth, I was thoroughly confused. Nothing made any sense. My entire investigation had fallen to pieces.

In deepest despair, I curled up beside the spare tire, closed my eyes, listened to the hum of the motor. I was bushed. It had been a long day, and one I would do my best to forget.

Slim drove north to the county road, then turned east. I didn't know where we were going and I didn't care. After all I'd been through, spending a few days in the back of a pickup seemed a pretty good deal.

Slim sped up and went through his gears. The rumble and bump of the caliche road beneath the tires was like music, and I felt myself drifting off and surrendering my iron grip on the world. Since I was in a rather low frame of mind, I chose a Bone Dream instead of the usual Beulah Dream. I cued it up and settled back to watch.

It was pretty good. Singing T-bones, thirteen of 'em in a long line of . . .

The hum of the tires changed pitch. So did the motor. We were slowing down.

Anyway, there was this line of singing T-bones, see, and . . .

The pickup pulled over to the side of the road and stopped. Slim's door opened. He stepped out and slammed the door. Gravel crunched beneath his feet.

He spoke. "Howdy. Are you having trouble?"

A man's voice answered. "Howdy, neighbor. Yes sir, this old pickup just quit on me."

"Uh-huh. You from around here?"

"No sir, just passing through the country. I'm from Oklahoma, over around Snaky Bend on the Canadian River. Ever been there?"

"Nope. I've heard they make moonshine whiskey over there."

"Heh. I've heard that myself, but I can't hardly believe it."

"What you got in the camper?"

"Say what?"

"You got anything in your camper?"

"Oh, that. No sir, just my camping stuff. Tools. Spare tire. Junk. You in the market for a camper?"

"Nope. Just curious. There's been some saddles stolen around here."

"No! Well, ain't that terrible! This world just seems to get wickeder and wickeder. People don't have respect for nothing anymore."

"Yalp. What seems to be wrong with your pickup?"

"Well, it quit. All at once, it just quit, like it wasn't getting gas or spark."

"I'm not much of a mechanic, but pop the hood and let's take a look."

"I'd sure appreciate that." They raised the hood. Then the stranger said, "Well, lookie here. I've got a couple of pieces of chocolate candy left. Here you go."

"Thanks."

"They're kindly hard to chew. Sure would gum up a set of false teeth."

HUH?

Sure would gum up a set of false teeth?

My head shot up and I came flying out of my dream about the dancing T-bones. Unless I was badly mistaken, I had just been given an opportunity to redeem myself.

I flew over the tailgate, hit the ground, and peeked around the back of the pickup.

The stranger was facing east, with his back to

me, so I couldn't see his face. But I saw that he was a small man with a slim build, that he wore sneakers on his feet and a blue-and-white cap on his head.

That was enough for me. The pieces of the puzzle were finally falling into place: the cap, the shoes, the pickup with a camper on the back, and most of all, the chocolate candy. That was the clincher right there, the chocolate candy—and his comment about how it would gum up a pair of false teeth. The same words, the exact same words, he'd used in the saddle shed.

All at once I felt the juices pumping again. New life and excitement surged through my entire body. I'd had enough of guilt and depression, hanging my head and dragging myself around like an . . . I don't know what. A whipped dog, I suppose, although no one had actually whipped me.

My confidence returned, that's the point. Mother Luck had brought this scoundrel back to me, and this time he wouldn't get away. Or if he did, it would be over my dad's body.

Dead body. Over my dead body.

Somehow I had to get the message to Slim, who was draped over the front of the pickup, scowling at the motor. Now, wasn't that something? Everyone on the ranch had made a big deal about me watching the thief empty the saddle shed, and we'd heard a lot of talk about me being a dumb dog, right? Well, here was Slim—helping the guy fix his pickup so that he could make his getaway! Oh well. We would deal with that later. I had to warn him, that was the main point.

Slim said, "Get in and hit the starter. I'll see if we're gettin' fire to the spark plugs."

The crook turned and started for the pickup door, and I got a good look at his face. It was the same guy: the beady little eyes, the sharp nose, the stringy moustache, and the Richardson Seeds cap.

Just then, he saw me. Our eyes met. In that small space of time, I read his thoughts. He recognized me. He knew I recognized him. And then it occurred to him that Slim worked for the very ranch he had robbed only a few hours before.

His eyes darted from side to side. He licked his lips and gave me a kind of sour grin. Then he spoke to Slim.

"Say, friend, is that your dog?"

Slim peered around the hood. "Yalp. That's Hank."

His gaze went from Slim to me and back to Slim. "You know, if you've got other things to do, I can fix this old pickup myself. I hate to take a man away from his business, know what I mean?"

"That's okay. Hit the starter."

"Does that dog ever bite?"

"Heh. Nope, not even when he's supposed to."

He squeezed up a smile. "Hi there, poochie. What's your name? Hank? You wouldn't bite a poor old cobbler from Oklahoma, would you?" Not unless I got the chance. "Now, I'm going to crawl in the pickup and you just stay where you're at, hear?"

I showed him some fangs. He reached two fingers into his shirt pocket and pulled out the roll of candy. He peeled off a piece and held it up.

"How about some candy, huh? I'll bet you just love chocolate candy."

Nope. Not interested.

His smile remained fixed. "I'll pitch it to you, how 'bout that, hmm? Can you catch it in the air? I bet you can. Here."

He pitched the candy in my direction. I didn't even look at it. My eyes were locked on the crook. The candy hit the ground and rolled up against my foot. All at once I caught a whiff of ... well, milk chocolate, creamy smooth milk chocolate and chewy caramel, and I must admit ... one little piece of chocolate wouldn't hurt, would it?

My nose was being pulled downward, as though by some powerful force. I tried to resist the pow-

erful magnetic force and set all the muscles in my
neck against it. No, no! I couldn't allow myself to
yield. I had to . . . but the force was so strong . . .

I Solve the Case, Capture the Crook, and Become a Hero

You probably think I gobbled it down, right? Fell for his chocolate trick the second time? Well, you're wrong.

You know what saved me? It wasn't the muscles in my neck or my powers of will. What saved me was the wicked light that danced in his eyes when he saw me going for the candy. *He thought he had found my fatal weakness and that he could beat me twice with the same trick.*

He thought wrong. You can fool Hank the Cowdog once in a row, but never twice in a row. At least, not with the same trick.

I sniffed the candy, picked it up in my mouth,

rolled it around several times . . . and let it fall back to the ground. Then I showed him a mouthful of fangs.

You should have seen his face. It just crumbled!

Slim broke the silence. "Hey, what's going on? Hit the starter."

"You know, bud, I . . . I think your dog wants to bite me, I do. Dogs don't like me. I don't know what it is."

"He won't bite, believe me."

In a flash, the guy made his move—opened the door and jumped inside. I made a lunge at him but was half a step too slow. He shook a finger at me and grinned. "Now be nice, Rover." Then he hit the starter.

"EEEEE-YOW!"

That was Slim. He let out a squall and banged his head against the hood. He came around the front of the pickup, rubbing his head with his hat still on. "Well, you're getting plenty of fire to the spark plugs, at least one of 'em." He noticed me sitting there beside the door, glaring daggers at the man inside—and trying, with every sign and gesture I could think of, to get the message across.

This is the crook. This is the guy who stole your saddles.

Slim studied me with a frown. "That's funny.

I've never seen him act this way around . . ." Then it hit him. I saw the light come on in his eyes. He rolled his gaze to the man in the pickup, then back to me. "Hank, do you know something I ought to know?"

I barked, fellers. I barked with all my heart and soul.

He patted me on the head. "Hmmm. It's worth checking."

Without saying another word, he walked around to the back of the pickup. I could have hugged him.

The thief knew he was in trouble. "Say, bud, the motor's up front. I wish you wouldn't . . ."

Slim opened the camper door. There was a moment of silence. Then, suddenly and all at once, the thief burst out the door and started running down the road.

I barked and waited for orders. Slim came at a run. "He's got the saddles, sure 'nuff, and I can't believe I almost . . . get 'im, Hank! I'll be right behind you."

Yes sir! That was the order I'd been waiting for. I hit the Afterburners, went to Full Throttle on all engines, and zoomed down the road after the enemy. It didn't take me long to catch up with him. He was running down the ditch now, fighting his way through tall sunflowers and Johnson grass.

He heard me coming and looked back over his shoulder. "Now poochie . . . now puppy . . . don't be bitter. Go chase a rabbit, hear? Get away from me, you fleabag!"

When I had closed the distance between us to ten yards, I began my Targeting Procedures. I took careful aim at his hip pockets, coaxed one last burst of speed out of the Afterburners, and . . . WHAMMO!

I nailed him, fellers, and once I had him on the ground, there was no way he was going to get away. He tried. He kicked and pushed and slapped and slugged and squalled naughty things about me. Heh, heh. I didn't care. It didn't matter what he did. He was MINE!

Slim was there in a flash. He'd lost his hat in the chase. His face was bright red and he was huffing and puffing. And somewhere along the way he'd picked up a cedar-post club about three feet long.

He put the end of the club down close to the thief's face. "Pardner, I'm making a citizen's arrest. You've got the right to resist, and if you do, I'll wrap this fence post around your ears and enjoy every minute of it."

The crook raised his hands. "Calf rope. Uncle. Peace, brother. I surrender, and can you call off this dog? I thought you said he wouldn't attack."

"Life's full of surprises, ain't it? Put your hands behind your back."

Slim tied his hands with baling twine and we hauled him back to headquarters. Loper called the law and Officers Hataway and Kile came back to collect Lester the Outlaw.

That was his name, Lester Somebody. He wasn't a poor cobbler, he didn't have five hungry children, and his wife didn't work at the Dairy Queen. He was well-known to law enforcement officers in Texas, Kansas, and Oklahoma. They'd been trying for months to catch him and . . .

I'm not one to criticize the work of our law enforcement personnel, but if they'd called *me* into the case a little sooner . . . oh well, things turned out well enough.

In fact, they turned out great. We got all the saddles and bridles back. I was restored to my position as Head of Ranch Security and—get this—received many pats on the head and thirteen "Good Dogs" from Sheriff Hataway and Deputy Kile. Pretty impressive, huh? You bet it was.

But even more heart-rendering was the ceremony on the front porch after the officers left the ranch. The Special Guest of Honor turned out to be . . . well, ME, you might say, and it turned out to be a very moving and emotional ceremony.

After disposing the ranch's Highest Award for Bravery upon me . . . bestowing, I should say . . . after the so-forth, Loper apologized for screeching at me and calling me hateful names.

And then—you won't believe this—Sally May herself delivered a long and touching speech about . . . okay, maybe it wasn't so long and maybe it wasn't so touching, but it was a speech . . . sort of.

What she said was that she was now willing to . . . how did she put it? She was now willing to "zero out" my "long list of sins, crimes, and buffoonery" and start all over with our relationship.

Does it get any better than that? Not on this ranch. And before we find out what Sally May meant by "baffoonery," let's shut 'er down and get some sleep.

Case cl . . .

Wait a minute, hold everything. I forgot about Jake. You're probably wondering what happened to him. Here's the deal.

After all the ceremonies and so forth were over, after the cheers of the crowd had faded into memories, Slim began wondering what had become of Jake.

After looking around for half an hour, he finally called me into the case. I led him straight to the pickup and pointed toward the tarp in the back.

He jerked it back and there was Jake, glaring at us. Guess what he said.

He said, "Get off this ship, you squids, or I'll have you walking the plank!"

About an hour later, a pickup rolled into headquarters. It was Jake's owner, a tall, skinny guy with a beard named Bill. That was the name of the man, not the beard. Beards don't . . . skip it. The point is that Jake was his dog.

Bill turned out to be a gold prospector from . . . somewhere . . . and he was looking for the long-lost King Solemnly's Mine. Loper explained that we were fresh out of gold mines on the ranch, and they left. As they drove away, Jake was standing up in the back of the pickup, like a captain looking out to sea.

And that's about the end of the story. Pretty good one, huh? You bet.

Case closed.

I just wish Beulah had been there.

Have you read all
of Hank's adventures?

Join Hank the Cowdog's Security Force

HANK THE COWDOG

Are you a big Hank the Cowdog fan? Then you'll want to join Hank's Security Force. Here is some of the neat stuff you will receive:

Welcome Package
- A Hank paperback embossed with Hank's top secret seal
- Free Hank bookmarks

Eight issues of *The Hank Times* with
- Stories about Hank and his friends
- Lots of great games and puzzles
- Special previews of future books
- Fun contests

More Security Force Benefits
- Special discounts on Hank books and audiotapes
- An original Hank poster (19" x 25") absolutely free
- Unlimited access to Hank's Security Force website at www.hankthecowdog.com

Total value of the Welcome Package and *The Hank Times* is $23.95. However, your two year membership is only **$8.95** plus $3.00 for shipping and handling.

To join Hank's Security Force, please send a check or money order for $11.95 ($8.95 plus $3.00 shipping and handling), payable to Maverick Books, to:

Hank's Security Force
Maverick Books
P.O. Box 549
Perryton, Texas 79070

Be sure to include your name, address, phone number, and your choice of a free book (choose from any book in the series). Please include two choices in case your first choice is out of stock.

DO NOT SEND CASH. NO CREDIT CARDS ACCEPTED.
Allow 4–6 weeks for delivery.

The Hank the Cowdog Security Force, the Welcome Package, and The Hank Times *are the sole responsibility of Maverick Books. They are not organized, sponsored, or endorsed by Penguin Putnam Inc., Puffin Books, Viking Children's Books, or their subsidiaries or affiliates.*

**Visit the fan club website at
www.hankthecowdog.com**

John R. Erickson

began writing stories in 1967 while working full-time as a cowboy, farmhand, and ranch manager in Texas and Oklahoma—where two of the dogs were Hank and his sidekick Drover. Hank the Cowdog made his debut a long time ago in the pages of *The Cattleman*, a magazine about cattle for adults. Soon after, Erickson began receiving "Dear Hank" letters and realized that many of his eager fans were children.

The Hank the Cowdog series won Erickson a *Publishers Weekly* "Listen Up" Award for Best Humor in Audio. He also received an Audie from the Audio Publishers Association for Outstanding Children's Series.

The author of more than thirty-five books, Erickson lives with his wife, Kris, and their three children on a ranch near his boyhood home of Perryton, Texas.

Gerald L. Holmes

met John Erickson after moving to Perryton, Texas, a long time ago . . . and that's when Hank and his pals came to life for the first time in pictures. Mr. Holmes has illustrated numerous cartoons and textbooks in addition to the Hank the Cowdog series.